Kain

The Splintered Hearts Series

Nicola Jane

Meet The Team

Cover design: Francessca Wingfield @ Wingfield Designs

Editor: Rebecca Vazquez, Dark Syde Books

Formatting: Nicola Miller

Spelling:

Please note, this author resides in the United Kingdom and is using British English. Therefore, some words may be viewed as incorrect or spelled incorrectly. However, they are not.

A note from the Author

This book contains cheating, heartbreak, and bad decisions. Things we can all relate to. Try not to take it to heart—the characters aren't real, and I made the story up in my head. But if you feel like it's vexing you too much, just stop reading.

Contents

Playlist   VII

CHAPTER ONE   1

CHAPTER TWO   6

CHAPTER THREE   14

CHAPTER FOUR   19

CHAPTER FIVE   29

CHAPTER SIX   42

CHAPTER SEVEN   50

CHAPTER EIGHT   58

CHAPTER NINE   66

CHAPTER TEN   76

CHAPTER ELEVEN   84

CHAPTER TWELVE   92

CHAPTER THIRTEEN   100

CHAPTER FOURTEEN   110

CHAPTER FIFTEEN   121

CHAPTER SIXTEEN		128
CHAPTER SEVENTEEN		135
CHAPTER EIGHTEEN		142
CHAPTER NINETEEN		150
CHAPTER TWENTY		159
CHAPTER TWENTY-ONE		168
CHAPTER TWENTY-TWO		179
CHAPTER TWENTY-THREE		186
CHAPTER TWENTY-FOUR		189
1.	Tanner - The Splintered Hearts Series	192
2.	More books from Nicola Jane	206

Playlist

One More Try – George Michael

I Can't Make You Love Me – Adele

Mixed Signals – Ruth B

Everything I Didn't Say – Ella Henderson

A Soulmate Who Wasn't Meant To Be – Jess Benko

Wicked Game – Daisy Gray (Cover)

Bad For Me – Meghan Trainor ft Teddy Swims

Tell Her You Belong To Me – Beth Hart

Why – Annie Lennox

Nothing Compares 2 U – Sinéad O'Connor

Trouble - Coldplay

Hold My Hand – Lady Gaga

You can listen here:

https://open.spotify.com/user/omqkvqsa4uybu790ss5iluv1y?si=O
N1gxsopQDSuRWuBd8BA6g&utm_source=copy-link

CHAPTER ONE

Kain

Cooper stares into the eyes of each and every one of us. "Mila's only just begun to talk to her family again, and I don't want to give them any reasons to think I'm not good enough for their daughter." He pauses and then turns to Tanner. "No drama with Brook," he warns, pointing a finger in his face. Tanner tries to hide his sheepish grin.

Marshall laughs, which brings Cooper's attention to him. "And you can stay the hell away from Harper today." Marshall's smile disappears, and I bite my inner cheek to stop me grinning from ear to ear. Serves the fucker right. He's been after my ex-hook-up for weeks now, and despite my fist hitting his face on more than one occasion, he still hasn't taken the hint.

Harper's pregnant with my kid. It wasn't planned, but we were happy to carry on with the hook-ups, until she tried to reveal her pregnancy to my ol' lady. Since then, I've kept my distance. "I don't want him upsetting," he adds, pointing in my direction.

Cooper, our club President, takes a minute to look around the semi-circle of brothers awaiting his further instruction. He's marrying Mila today, the woman he was always supposed to be with despite life getting in the way on a few occasions. He's nervous, not that he'll admit it, but I can tell by the way his fingers twitch and by the rants that he keeps reigning down on the brothers.

Mila wanted a huge wedding this time around. She's not usually the type to be a diva and make demands, but the last time Cooper was supposed to marry her, his ex returned, ruining their plans. Mila was taking no prisoners this time. She insisted that if Cooper wanted to marry her so badly, then he could spend his money on a big white wedding. That way, if he decided to let her down again, he was out of pocket a good few grand. Cooper isn't one for fuss, preferring to marry her in a quiet ceremony and then whisk her away on their honeymoon, but he needed to prove to her that he was serious this time around and that he wasn't going to fuck it all up again.

"Brothers, I need this day to go without a glitch. If you spot something about to go off, then you need to squash it. No drama, no fighting, no fucking." We all snigger at that one. Mila has cousins and friends coming who haven't met us before, and she's already warned us that no one from the MC can hit on them.

We take turns slapping our President on the back and wish him luck. The brothers step out the back room and into the church, leaving me and Cooper alone.

He begins to pace, and I smirk. "You nervous she's gonna leave your arse standing there this time?" I joke, and he glares at me, his expression anything but amused. "Relax, Coop, I was kidding," I say. "Mila loves you. She's gonna be there."

_ ℓℓ _

Checking my watch, it's a few minutes after when Mila should have arrived and Cooper is twitching. "Call her and find out where the fuck she is," he growls, close to my ear. The church is packed out with no seating space. Mila really did go all out on the invites. I spot Harper's parents towards the back of the church. They don't know me, but I've seen their pictures around Harper's place. Rich and pompous is how she described them.

"I'll go and take a look outside. Relax," I whisper.

Stepping out into the church grounds, I breathe a sigh of relief when I spot a white Rolls Royce coming to a stop at the entrance. The driver gets out and rushes to open the passenger door. I watch as Harper steps out in a long, silk lilac gown that's fitted perfectly to her gorgeous pregnant figure. She wobbles on the heels, and the driver steadies her, causing my eyes to zone in to where their hands connect, and I scowl. I hate any man touching her to the point I want to break his damn fingers, but she'll only remind me she doesn't belong to me.

She might be pregnant with my kid, but we've done too much to each other to ever make things right between us. When she texted Ginger to break the news that she was pregnant, I was furious. Not only because Ginger is also pregnant, but because Harper was the one who told me she wasn't interested in me and that I should live my life with Ginger. Women are so confusing.

Harper's eyes connect with mine and that familiar burning in my chest flickers to life. I love everything about this woman, from her gorgeous bright blues to her perky little backside. She keeps me on my toes with her fiery temperament, and I find it hard to resist that usual pull that draws me to her whenever she's nearby. My body craves her, but her blank expression soon brings me back down to Earth. It's like she's flipped a switch and now she looks at me with nothing—not love, not even hate, just nothing.

"Is Mila on her way, because Cooper's in there busting a nut with stress," I say light heartedly.

"Yes, she's in the car behind us. She should be here any second," she says politely, and I hate that indifference in her tone.

Brook is next to step from the car in a dress matching Harper's. She smiles wide when she sees me. Tanner's ol' lady is something else, always laughing and smiling. She reaches up to me and kisses my cheek. "You look so handsome, Kain," she says, rubbing her lipstick stain from my cheek.

"Damn, lady, if you weren't with Tanner, I'd be all over this arse today," I say with a wink, and she playfully taps my shoulder. "Don't tell Tanner I said that," I add. That guy is bat shit crazy when it comes to Brook, and he'd beat my arse before he heard me out.

I head back inside, and Cooper looks up with a hope that soon fades when he realises it's just me. As best man, I should mess with his head a little, but I can see the guy is in pain with nerves, so I pat him on the shoulder. "They're arriving now. Photos and all that," I say, and he sucks in a deep breath, nodding.

A few minutes later, the music begins and everyone stands. I take my place by Cooper's side as we move to the front. I turn and watch as the bridesmaids begin their descent down the aisle towards us. I can't help but admire Harper's beauty, and the fact that her perfectly rounded pregnant stomach makes her even more beautiful to me. My heart squeezes, and I wonder if this would eventually have been us if we hadn't messed it all up. I've never considered marriage before, but I would for her. I feel eyes burning into the side of my face and I see Ginger watching me carefully. I smile at her, but she doesn't return it. She's obviously noticed me staring at Harper. I'll pay for that later, I'm sure.

CHAPTER TWO

Harper

Why does he insist on staring at me like that? Before, when no one knew about us, it was sexy and appealing, but now, it makes me want to slap him hard across the face. Ginger will no doubt have noticed because she's like a damn hawk-eye whenever we're all in the same room together. She doesn't know this baby is his, but I think she suspects. She'll never voice that out loud and face up to it though, not if it means she might lose Kain.

I take my place across the altar from Kain and Cooper. Glancing back, I watch my best friend since forever walk towards her future. She looks amazing in her Vera Wang wedding gown. I laughed when she told us she was having such a large wedding cos it wasn't Mila's usual style, but I'm pleased she went big. Not only does she look stunning, but the whole day so far has been magical. We've all been pampered and preened to within an inch of our lives. It's the first time I've ever looked at myself in the mirror and gasped.

ele

The ceremony is beautiful, and my face hurts from the smile I have plastered on my face. There's just something about weddings that brings out the happiness inside me.

We gather outside for photographs. The church grounds are picturesque, and Mila's paid extra to have some photos taken despite Cooper's protests about him being too big and bad to have photos. I stand patiently while we are swapped back and forth, pictures taken with the bride and groom, pictures taken with just the bride and bridesmaids . . . the list is endless, and I can feel my ankles beginning to swell. Marshall stands just behind me. "Baby, you look so hot," he whispers, and I smile to myself.

Marshall is one of the brothers from the Hammers MC. Before I realised that I was pregnant, he was a hook-up. At first, I used him just as much as he did me. I needed to get over Kain, and he needed to fuck—it was that simple. Kain became jealous, and once the news of my pregnancy came to light, I've tried to tone down the flirting. Kain begged me not to get with any of the club brothers, and although he doesn't deserve my word, I don't want to upset him because we've caused each other far too much pain as it is.

"Back away, Marshall," I mutter, hardly moving my lips, and he laughs.

"I'm on my best behaviour today. Cooper warned us all before the wedding, but I just wanted to tell you that I think you look amazing and that you're the only pregnant woman I've ever looked at and gotten a hard-on," he says. I laugh out loud and watch as he saunters away. I catch Kain's eye, he's unhappy about the exchange, I can read it on his face, but I'm not going to ignore Marshall completely. We're still friends.

"Okay, can I have Harper and Kain," shouts Mila, and I wince. This will cause problems between Kain and Ginger, and I have no doubts that Mila's done this on purpose. I take a deep breath and make my way to the large oak tree. I stand on Mila's side, and Kain moves to Cooper's side. We smile for the photographer, and he clicks away before Mila steps away, pulling Cooper with her. I glare at her, and she smiles at us innocently.

"I'd like a picture of my best friend and Cooper's Vice President," she says, and then she lowers her tone. "Besides, don't you want one picture that you can show your child once it's here?" she adds, and a pang of guilt hits me.

My child will have to share his or her daddy with a child just one month older than itself. The thought has kept me awake at night, and as awful as it is, I've often wondered if I've made the right decision by keeping this baby. I subconsciously place my hand on my tiny little bump, and Kain moves next to me, placing an arm around my waist and tucking me closer to him. I force an awkward smile, mainly because I can feel Ginger's eyes on us and I know she must feel so much hatred towards me. She won't cause an issue because she has no solid evidence other than knowing we had a thing before she came back into Kain's life, but as a woman, she must sense it. I must set off her alarm bells whenever I'm near her man.

"Are you feeling okay? We've been standing around for a long time," he whispers, and I nod. I don't tell him that my feet hurt bad but I can't bend to remove my shoes, or that my back is also hurting, because he'll try and take care of that for me, and I don't want questions coming from Ginger. Not on Mila's day. Once the photographer gives us the nod, I move away from Kain quickly and make my way through the crowd.

I feel my father's eyes on me as I approach. I didn't want them here today, but Mila's mother insisted on inviting them. They've been friends since Mila and I were born, although they don't tend to see each other these days, not unless there's a special occasion like this.

"Sweetie, you look lovely," says my mother, kissing my cheeks.

"Seven months already," my father mutters, also swooping down to kiss my cheek. I shudder involuntary and fold my arms over my chest before stepping back from him.

"Are you staying for the party, or do you have to jet off?" I ask hopefully. My father is always flying off for business, and usually my mother goes with him.

"Actually, we'll be staying around for the next week or so. It seems odd being in the house and not a hotel." My mother smiles. "We don't have to be anywhere until the end of next week, so I can spend some time with you," she adds excitedly.

"Yay," I mutter with less enthusiasm, but my mother doesn't react. I don't know if that's because she doesn't understand my sarcasm or she just doesn't care.

"Harper, I had the accountant put some money into your bank this week. Have you received it?" asks my father. I nod and force a smile. He often deposits money into my account, but I never touch it. I don't want his guilt money, but I don't tell him that. Instead, I pretend I've spotted someone important and make my excuses to leave.

I ease the shoes from my swollen feet and haul my legs up so I can rest them on the seat next to me. I glance around the large white tent decorated with twinkling lights and fake flickering candles. Mila hired a team of people to put up the tent on the clubhouse grounds so the guys could drink themselves stupid and then not have far to crawl to their beds. Plus, she reasoned no hotel would be happy with a bunch of rowdy bikers partying in their establishment. Looking around, you wouldn't know we were at the clubhouse.

Marshall approaches and takes a seat next to my feet. "Your cankles giving you grief?" he jokes, and I scowl at his name for my swollen ankles.

"Why aren't you drinking shots and chatting up Mila's family?" I ask, and he shrugs his huge shoulders.

He trails a finger over the top of my foot and then looks me direct in the eyes. "They don't interest me, Harper," he says seriously. "Not like you do."

"Marshall, don't," I warn. "We talked about this. It was fun, but as you can see, I have other priorities now," I say, pointing to my bump.

"I can't help how I feel, baby." He sighs, taking my foot in his large hand and gently massaging it. I close my eyes because this seriously feels better than sex right now. My brain is telling me to stop him, but my poor feet are screaming in delight as he rubs away the pain.

"Marshall, did you not hear the Pres today?" asks Kain, his shadow looming over us. I sigh and open one eye as Marshall gently places my foot back on the chair.

"Yes, VP, I did. I was just helping her out," Marshall says, standing.

"Well, that ain't your job, is it?" asks Kain firmly, and Marshall salutes him before walking away. "Cheeky fucker." He sighs, taking the seat that Marshall vacated. "If you're tired, why don't I get one of the prospects to take you home?"

"Because it's my best friend's wedding, and we still have," I look at my watch, "an hour before she leaves for the airport."

"There's lots of bedrooms free here if you want to stay over," he offers, and I shake my head. The last time I stayed here at the clubhouse, we ended up starting an affair.

"How's Ginger coping?" She's a month further on than me, and I noticed she's carrying her weight differently. Kain fidgets, which he does a lot when he's uncomfortable, but I'm trying to make this whole situation easier on us both. I don't want to be bitter and jealous, and I don't want to be the other woman anymore. I made it clear from the beginning of my pregnancy that I'm not expecting anything from Kain. I chose to keep the baby, and by that time, he'd already announced Ginger's pregnancy. Once he found out about me, he tried to come crawling back, but it felt like a pity thing rather than love, and I was sick of being his second choice.

"Ginger is fine," he says, his tone clipped.

I sigh. "I'm not asking to be a bitch, Kain. I was being polite."

"Well, it's weird, my knock-off asking about my ol' lady." The words sting, but I cover it well. He's never referred to Ginger as his ol' lady, not to me anyway.

He realises what he's said and runs a hand over his neatly trimmed beard. "Sorry, I didn't mean it like that. It's not official. Ginger and I haven't said it . . ." He trails off. "Anyway, I came over here because—"

This time, I cut him off. "Because you saw Marshall talking to me," I say coldly. I know his game, always ready to intercept any potential lovers. He must think low of me if he thinks I'd be having sex with Marshall right now at seven months pregnant.

"Well, that too, but no. I came to see if you need anything for the baby. Cooper mentioned that you'd asked for extra shifts behind the bar. I know babies cost a lot. Ginger's spent a fortune kitting out the bedroom and . . ." He trails off again, and this time, he winces, realising his words are messed up again.

Working at the clubhouse bar is ideal, but it doesn't pay great, and although I've been saving throughout the pregnancy, I need the extra cash for the baby things that I'll be needing soon. "No, it's fine. I have everything." I stand abruptly, grimacing as my feet pinch. I grip my shoes in one hand and my bag in the other. "See you around," I say brightly, and I go to find Mila. I shouldn't be upset. It was my choice to step away from the whole situation, and I honestly think Kain would have stepped up if I'd have let him, but I also think he'd have kept both me and Ginger, and I wasn't prepared to continue to be the other woman. I should never have been that in the first place.

My father grips me by the arm as I pass him, halting my steps. "Why haven't you touched any of the money in your account?" he hisses. I pull my wrist free and rub it.

"Because I've told you over and over that I don't want your hush money. I have a job."

"It isn't hush money. Don't be so dramatic." He takes a calming breath before adding, "Gloria would like you to come over for lunch tomorrow, and I told her you'll be there."

I groan and don't bother to hide it. The fact that my parents will be in the same town as my stepmother is awkward and I can't relax. "I don't want to come over for lunch. Why can't you leave me out of it?" I snap.

"I'll send a car to collect you at twelve," he says, kissing me on the forehead. "I've booked your mother into a health spa. She needs a rest." *Of course, you have,* I think to myself bitterly.

CHAPTER THREE

Kain

I watch the exchange between Harper and her father from where I'm stood at the bar. I don't like the look of him. Maybe I'm biased because of the way Harper has spoken about him, but to me, he looks sleezy and too self-assured for his own good.

"People will begin to think you're her stalker if you continue to watch her from a distance." Brook appears by my side and gently nudges me with her shoulder. Her small frame doesn't have the desired affect and I don't budge.

"To know that I'm watching her, you'd have to be watching me," I say playfully, smirking down at her.

She throws her head back and laughs aloud, then she brings her eyes to me. "Seriously, Kain, what happened between you guys? It hurts my heart to see the longing in your eyes. You love her."

I laugh and roll my eyes. Damn women love a romance story. "I don't do love. She's carrying my kid, so of course, I'm watching out for her."

"Is that what you tell yourself?" she asks thoughtfully. "Does it help you to cope with the situation better?"

"Where is Tanner? Shouldn't he have spotted you talking to another male by now and come over here all steam coming from his nostrils to throw you over his shoulder?"

I'm not exaggerating, because even though most of the brothers are loyal in the club and we wouldn't dream of hitting on another's ol' lady, Tanner would still react badly to us talking without him being present.

"You love her, and she loves you. Deny it all you want." Brook smiles smugly, like an irritating little sister.

"Actually, Brook, did she say anything to you about money? Cooper says she asked for extra bar shifts." Brook and Harper aren't really close like Mila is with each of the girls, but they may have talked about it amongst each other.

"She doesn't talk about that stuff to me, but I know she doesn't have anything for the baby yet." She shrugs. "Mila was getting on her back about sorting it out because she doesn't even have so much as a booty." That's what I suspected.

Ginger joins us, placing her hand possessively on my arse. "Are we going home yet? I'm exhausted." She wants to go home to fight. I know the signs, and she's been displaying them since the church when she caught me watching Harper.

"I was thinking of staying here tonight," I say, and her expression changes to pissed within a second.

"Well, you can take me home first," she says sharply.

"I've been drinking, babe. I can get a prospect to drop you," I suggest. I feel her grip my shirt from behind. She's getting angrier by the second.

"Fine, we'll stay here. Walk me to the room." She takes my hand in hers and leads me away from Brook.

As soon as we are out of earshot and walking up the stairs, she turns on me and slaps me hard across the cheek. "All fucking day I've watched you staring at her," she screams. I grip my cheek, the sting burning instantly. When she gets like this, it's best to stay quiet and ride it out.

"Can we at least get into the room?" I growl. She shoves me, her nails digging into my back, and I walk towards the room. I'm one step inside when she begins reigning blows down over me and screaming profanities about Harper. I manage to reach for the door and slam it closed to stop passing brothers witnessing the impending argument. "Be careful of the baby," I grate out.

"Like you care about this baby," she screams, throwing her shoe towards me. I dodge it, but then the other comes flying, catching me in the eye.

"Ginger, calm down. It's not good for the baby," I warn her again.

"If you want that whore so bad, then go to her," she yells. I try to take her hand, but she slaps me again, and I clench my teeth, trying to remain calm.

"I don't want her. I want you." It doesn't matter how many times I say this to her, when she's like this, she doesn't hear it.

"Lies! Always fucking lies," she screams. "You think I'm stupid, that I don't see it, but I know. I see you with her." I feel wetness on my cheek, and I wipe at it with the back of my hand to find blood. Her shoe must have cut me. "Go back to her. Get out and go to her and her bastard child." She always refers to Harper's unborn child as a bastard because when she asked me who the father was, I told her that Harper didn't know. It was a shit thing to do because I could have said anything other than making Harper out like she was some kind of club whore. But Ginger had put me on the spot, and I hadn't prepared my lies well enough back then.

I reach for her again, and this time, she lets me pull her towards me. I wrap my arms around her, and she sobs into my chest. "I love you. Just you," I say over and over while I stroke circles over her back. Her hands go to my face, and for a split second, I'm not sure if she's going to scratch me, so I tense, but she pulls my face down to meet hers and kisses me gently. These times, when we fight like this, I feel less turned on and more depressed, but if I make an excuse to try and deter her, she will only get upset again.

I run my fingers through her hair and grip a handful at the roots. I tug it slightly harder than I normally would, still pissed about the cut and the fact that my cheek is on fire from her slap. Walking her backwards until we reach the bed, I turn her away from me, pull up her long dress, and guide her to bend slightly, pulling her panties down to her knees. I press my hand to her wet entrance and wonder if it's the violence that turns her on or my touch. I don't bother with foreplay, I'm tired and the blood from my cut is dripping from my jawline, causing a mess. I grip my semi-hard erection and press it to her entrance, hoping to God I can make it harder with a little friction.

I close my eyes as I start to move in and out, happy that with a picture of Harper in my mind, I'm able to get hard enough to fuck

Ginger. It's another argument averted. I reach around to her front and press my finger against her clit. I need to make this quick—my cut is throbbing and I'm feeling dizzy. She cries out and her legs begin to shake as she climaxes. I follow shortly after, mainly from the relief that I've released into her and that'll make her happy for now.

In all the madness last night, I didn't close the curtains, so the sun wakes me. I glance to my left where Ginger lies naked beside me, then I get up and close them. She needs the rest after her outburst and all the time we spent making up through the night. I sigh when I see her arms and legs are covered in bruises. Her skin is pale, so the bruises stand out.

I catch sight of myself in the mirror. My eye is bruised, and the cut is just below it with dried blood running down my cheek. I have welts on my neck where Ginger sucked hard to mark me. It placates her, so I don't argue or fuss about it.

I shower and dress as quietly as possible so as not to wake her and then I head downstairs to see what kind of mess the clubhouse is in. As Vice President, I'm in charge for the next two weeks while Cooper is away on his honeymoon. I'm pleased to see the prospects have already begun the tidy-up, so I head to the office to make some calls and get a plan in action to get some things for Harper's baby.

CHAPTER FOUR

Harper

"This isn't for me," I say, looking down at the clipboard that the delivery guy thrusts towards me. There's a list of baby things that I know I haven't ordered.

"You are Harper Banks?" asks the guy.

"Well, yes, but I haven't ordered any of this," I repeat. He shrugs, his expression telling me he couldn't give a rat's arse if I ordered it because he's delivering it whether I sign for it or not. He holds out his pen and raises his eyebrows at me. I sigh and snatch the pen, scribbling something that vaguely resembles my signature on the dotted line. The guy gives two other men waiting by the truck a nod to unload the items.

Ten minutes later, I'm staring at the boxes piled in my living room and wondering what the hell I'm going to do with all this stuff. When there's a knock at the door, I open it cautiously because who the hell knows what's coming next. Two prospects, Irish and Curt, stand there with decorating equipment. "Hey," I say, confused.

"Kain sent us. We're here to decorate the baby's room," says Irish. Suddenly, the pieces slot into place and I groan aloud. I don't want Kain's involvement to be this. I don't want his money because it feels like he's buying my silence, just like my father.

"And if I tell you no?" I ask, because I know Kain will have given them strict instructions.

"Then we're to call him and, in his words, he'll beat the fuck out of us until you let us in." I nod and open the door wider. I know that Kain would do that, and he knows I'd hate it, so there's no point in arguing. I decide that I'll go and see him after I've had lunch with my father and Gloria.

I park my car outside the large home that Gloria believes she shares with my father. I make sure to plaster a smile on my face so that my father doesn't have any reason to pick an argument with me. My stepmum opens the door and looks genuinely pleased to see me, which makes the guilt so much worse. I kiss her warmly on the cheek before following her inside. My father is washing vegetables at the kitchen sink and the bitterness kicks in. He'd never do that with my mum.

"Here she is, my gorgeous girl." He smiles. *He makes my skin crawl with his smarmy lies.* "Wow, you're getting big," he adds, looking at my stomach like he's surprised, because Gloria would assume that my father has been away on business up until today, and so he wouldn't have seen me.

"Seven months now, isn't that right?" asks Gloria, and I nod. "And we still haven't met the handsome man responsible?" That's where my lies have come in. I guess the apple really doesn't fall far from the tree, but I know my father and he would not approve of Kain, or any biker for that matter. He'd bring all kinds of trouble to the club, and I don't want that.

"I'm sorry, he's away on business, trying to close a deal in Mexico," I lie, and Gloria gives me a sympathetic smile.

"Oh, I know how that feels," she says with a laugh and a wink to my father.

I'm almost knocked over as the twins race in to see me, throwing their arms around my legs, both chatting at the same time. Gloria warns them to calm down because of the baby, but I don't mind them. They're the only reason I put up with this charade. Libby and Bella have just turned five years old, but my father's affair stretches way back before the girls were born.

"Anton is coming too, and he's bringing us presents," screams Libby excitedly. I glare at my father, guilt written all over his face.

"How lovely," I say, and he gives me an apologetic shrug. "Let's go upstairs and see what toys you have for us to play with today," I add, wanting to get out of there before Anton turns up. Anton is Gloria's eldest son from a previous marriage, one my father broke up, and Anton seems to hold a grudge towards me and my father, even though I never agreed with any of this. When Gloria announced her pregnancy six years ago, it tipped Anton over the edge, and now, he treats me like something he stepped in.

I spend an hour hiding upstairs before he appears. His suit and tie for dinner with his mother is a bit too much, and I'm pretty sure he does it to try and prove that he's important and we are superior to him. He owns a few businesses, and though I tend to switch off whenever he talks about himself, which is a lot, I know they're something to do with property and he makes a lot of money.

"Lunch is ready," he says, glaring down at me playing Legos on the girls' bedroom floor. Both twins throw themselves at him, and he hands them each a gift bag. They sit down and begin ripping into them, each pulling out a Barbie doll at the same time and screaming with delight. Anton smiles at them fondly, and I think we can both agree that the twins are the only good thing that's come from my father.

"Can you get up from down there?" he asks, screwing his face up at my bump. I scowl and push myself into a kneeling position before standing and straightening my summer dress. "No sign of the mystery donor?"

"He's working away," I say quietly, knowing full well that Anton doesn't buy my bullshit story about the rich father of my child.

"Huh, of course, he is," he mutters.

We sit at the dinner table and, as always, Gloria has provided a feast. Creamed potatoes and other vegetables are in dishes in the centre of the table. My father carves the roast beef at the head of the table while the rest of us pile vegetables and potatoes on our plates.

"How's work?" Gloria asks me. She thinks I work as a self-employed accountant, as do both my parents.

"It's fine," I mutter. The lies build higher, and it makes me choke. "Busy," I add.

"I thought I saw you the other day, near that old, abandoned warehouse. I think some motorcycle gang owns it now," says Anton smugly.

"Yes, I sometimes look over books for the bar there," I lie, and Anton laughs and shakes his head. It crosses my mind to ask how he saw me because the clubhouse is tucked away at the very back of an industrial estate, hidden behind a large, abandoned factory, but I want to move off the subject quickly.

"I don't think that's a good idea. It's bad enough that Mila's gone and gotten herself involved with them, you need to steer clear," warns my father.

I sigh, pushing the vegetables around on my plate. "It's my job."

"You sure the baby's daddy isn't one of those MC guys?" asks Anton. "It would explain why you don't want us to meet him." I wait for Gloria to jump in and tell Anton to lay off me, but I find her looking at me like she's interested in the answer.

"Of course not," I snap, blushing.

"Honey, if it is, you don't need to hide it from us," says Gloria kindly.

"To hell she doesn't," snaps my father.

"It's not anyone from the MC, Christ." I groan, stuffing potatoes in my mouth.

As soon as dinner is over, I make my excuses to leave. I need to see Kain about the baby room fiasco. My father walks me to the door, his face stern. "Is it a biker, Harper?" he hisses.

"No," I repeat. "It's just Anton causing trouble as usual."

"Your mother wants to meet for lunch later in the week. We'll meet you on your lunch hour and you will bring the baby's father."

"Where does Gloria think you'll be?" I ask snidely, and he slaps me across the face, grabbing my upper arm. He likes to be hands-on towards me and my mother, always looking at us with resentment, yet he's never laid a finger on Gloria, which I'm pleased about, of course. I just don't get why he's like this towards us.

"I'll text you with the details. And, Harper, I suggest you learn to control your tongue, or your mother will pay the price." I pull free from his grip and walk fast towards my car. It's not until I'm safely inside that I cry. I never let my father see me cry.

When I get to the clubhouse, there are removal trucks parked out front to take away the wedding decorations and tent. It's almost like there was never even a wedding. Sam glances up from his newspaper when I enter. "I didn't know you were on shift today," he says.

"I'm not. Where's Kain?" I ask. Sam points to the clubhouse door at the back of the bar, and I head that way. There're a few of the guys hanging out. Tanner acknowledges me and then goes back to watching the television. I knock on Cooper's office door, and Kain shouts for me to come in. He's sat behind the desk, staring down at his mobile phone, and when he looks up, I gasp. His eye is bruised and there's a cut just under it.

"What happened to you?" I ask.

"It's nothing, messing with the guys," he says with a smile. "What can I do for you?"

"I don't want the furniture you sent me, Kain," I start, but he puts a hand up to stop me.

"That's not up for discussion. It's my baby too, and I'm entitled to pay for the baby shit you'll need."

"I really don't want to argue with you, but the stuff is going back. I've got it covered."

He stands abruptly, and I automatically move back. His face softens and he sighs. "Don't step back from me like I beat on you." He wouldn't understand that it's an automatic reaction after years of seeing violence from my father, and the fact that I've already had a slap today. "It's too late to send the stuff back. the guys have started putting it together."

"Well, then, I'll pay you back." I sigh. I'm exhausted, and the baby is non-stop moving today, constantly pushing on my bladder. I wince when it takes another kick, and Kain rushes to me, gently guiding me to the couch to sit down.

"Look, I don't want you to pay me back. Please let me buy this stuff for my child. It's the least I can do."

"As long as you agree that from now on, if you want to buy anything, you run it by me first," I say, and Kain nods in agreement. I notice the marks on his neck, and he catches me staring.

"Is that everything?" he asks, standing. This is his way of avoiding me asking awkward questions, but I don't want to know because it's quite clear to me that he's moved on and he's happy. I stand and move towards the door.

"At some point, we need to sit down and talk about what you want from all of this," I say. He approaches me from behind and presses his hand on the door to keep me from opening it.

"Go on," he says.

"Well, will you just visit? Do you even want to see the baby, or would you prefer not to?" I ask. It's all things that we've argued about at one point or another, but we've never sat down and talked properly. Now the time is getting closer, it feels like it's something we should do.

"Of course, I want to see the baby. Do I need to set a time and day?" he asks.

I think about it. I don't want him to turn up whenever he feels like it. I don't want him to be like my father. "Yes," I say, and he frowns. I turn to face him properly and lean back against the door. "I don't think it's fair for you to just turn up whenever you can fit the baby in. You'll be wanting to spend time with your child on your own, and I'll need to know when that is so I can make sure I haven't already made plans."

"I want to spend time with both of you, as a family," he states. This angers me because we aren't a family.

"No, that isn't what I want. It'll confuse the baby. You can have your time whenever you want, just let's make real arrangements so we both know where we stand," I suggest.

"Fuck that, Harper. You know what my life is like right now. I can't commit to times and days. Sometimes I'm on the road, and I'll have Ginger and the baby to consider."

"So, what do I do, sit around and wait 'til you show?" I snap. He's being unreasonable. I can't put my life on hold, and neither can our child.

"I don't know how it's gonna work, but it will. We'll sort it out."

"No, that's not enough. I want proper visitations set up or it won't be happening, so have a think about it and get back to me," I say, pulling the door open and leaving. He follows me, hot on my heels, and I can't deny it gives me a thrill. It reminds me of a time when he used to follow me and we'd argue, then it would lead to crazy, hot sex.

We stop in our tracks when Ginger steps in front of us. She looks between us both with her arms folded over her chest and a disapproving expression on her face. "What's going on?" she asks.

"I came to ask for more shifts. Seems Cooper didn't sort that out before he went off on his honeymoon," I say quickly, the lies rolling out so easily.

"Right," she mutters. "Well, actually, Kain needed to speak to you about that, didn't you, Kain," she says, glaring at him.

"I did?" he asks, surprise evident on his face.

"Yes. We think it's best you don't work any extra hours. In fact, Sam is coping pretty well without you, so maybe it's time you looked for another job," Ginger says firmly, not breaking eye contact with me.

"Oh, Cooper never said—" I begin, but she cuts in with a laugh, and her pitying look is condescending and has the desired effect. She's letting me know that she's part of this club and I'm not, therefore, she gets a say in whether I can stay or not.

"Well, seems Cooper forgot a lot of things. Maybe he didn't want to be the one to tell you seeing as you're his wife's BFF and all, but Kain isn't afraid to do Cooper's dirty work."

I turn to look at Kain, who is eyeing Ginger with what appears to be indecision, but his eyes eventually fall to me and he sighs. "Sorry, Harper, it's for the best."

My mouth falls open in shock. I need the job, or I'll be forced to live on my father's guilt money. "Kain, you can't do this. I need that job," I say.

Marshall approaches us, his expression concerned, and I hate that this little show of her dominance is getting attention from surrounding onlookers. "Everything okay, Harper?" he asks.

"No, I'm not okay. Kain's firing me from the bar. I need that money," I cry. Marshall places his arm around me, knowing Kain can't say anything without having to explain his actions to Ginger.

"Man, that's cold. She's seven months pregnant, who else will employ her?" asks Marshall.

"It's the way it's gotta be," grits out Kain, his eyes fixed on Marshall's arm.

"Does Sam know, or Cooper, for that matter?" Marshall questions.

Kain growls and rushes forward, gripping hold of Marshall and knocking me to the side. The sudden movement winds me and I hunch over to catch my breath. Tanner is by my side immediately, while Kain and Marshall shove at each other, seemingly oblivious to me.

"Last time I checked, I was the fucking VP, Marshall, so watch your damn mouth," yells Kain.

"When Cooper gets back, he's gonna kick your arse, and then he's gonna let Mila kick it too," yells Marshall, moving back towards me. He wraps an arm around my shoulders. "Are you okay?" he whispers gently, and I nod.

"Harper, I'm sorry, are you okay?" asks Kain, also moving towards me. Marshall tucks me closer into his side.

"Come on, baby, I'll take you home and look after you," says Marshall with a smug smile thrown in Kain's direction. I let him lead me from the clubhouse knowing Kain won't be allowed to run after me.

CHAPTER FIVE

Kain

Fuck, Harper hates me, and now, that smooth bastard, Marshall, is gonna step in there, and what the hell can I do about it? Yeah, I could order him to stay the fuck away, but as Cooper already pointed out, the brotherhood comes before women, and he won't stand for us fighting over a woman in this club. Ginger waits until the office door is closed before she punches me hard in the face. I'm not a small guy, but I refuse to hit a woman, and she knows that, which is why she tries to take a second punch. This time, I catch her wrist and pull her towards me.

"Stop," I growl, and for the first time, she looks at me stunned. I've never stopped her before. "You crossed the fucking line, Ginger. You stepped into club business, and Cooper will have my balls for this."

"I don't want her around you, and as an ol' lady, I have priority," she hisses. She's right, her needs do take priority over non-members, but I don't think this is a normal situation, and Cooper will not let this slide. This decision will upset his new wife and he won't be happy about that.

"It wasn't your decision. Cooper makes those orders, not some ol' lady of a club member. I can just about put up with your shit when it comes to you hitting out at me, but don't fuck with Harper's life," I snap. She slaps me hard with her free hand, her nails scratching into my cheek, and I inhale sharply. I play a mantra in my head, *'Don't hit her, don't hit her.'* "Fucking bitch," I hiss gently, shoving her from me.

"Go to her! Go to her," she screams, and I stand. *Fuck this bullshit.* But as I get to the door, Ginger loses her shit again and begins hitting herself in the stomach, screaming and yelling. I go back to her and grip her wrists in my hands, holding them until she calms down. Tear tracks mark her cheeks as she sobs. She's desperate, and I hate that I did this to her. I pull her to me and kiss her on the head, wrapping her tightly in my arms.

"We need to speak to the doctor, baby," I whisper into her hair, not bothering to hide the desperation in my voice. I know she doesn't want that, but I'm out of options. I feel her shake her head and I lift her face to look at me again. "It's going to be okay," I reassure her.

"No," she sniffles, "there's two weeks left. We can make two weeks, and then I can start the meds again. Stay away from her. It makes everything worse." She sobs, and I nod, agreeing to her small ask, and it is small considering everything she's doing for our baby. I place a kiss to her lips and wipe her tears away with my thumb. We can do two weeks.

Later that evening, I wait until Ginger falls asleep before driving over to Harper's. I need to clear shit up and then step away until Ginger has the baby and she can sort her head out.

I knock on the front door, noticing Marshall's bike is out front. He opens the door and gives a sarcastic laugh when he sees me. "I know I didn't scratch your face like some damn bitch, which means Ginger must have beat your arse." His smug smile annoys me instantly, but I take a calming breath.

I sigh, and ask in a bored tone, "Is she here?"

"Yeah. I was rubbing her feet while she sobs at a chick flick, but I don't know if I want you upsetting her again today. She's pretty fragile right now," he says thoughtfully.

"I'm not in the mood, brother. Do not stand in my way on this," I snarl, shoving past him and heading inside.

Harper is laying on the sofa, her feet up and a tissue in her hand. She's beautiful, even when she cries. "We need to talk," I say, Marshall standing by my side. "Alone," I add, just to clarify.

"There's nothing to say. You made yourself pretty clear."

"There's lots to say, so send this fucker packing."

"If anyone is packing, it'll be you," she snaps, pushing herself to stand. "The kitchen," she orders me, then she smiles at Marshall. "I won't be long." Harper closes the kitchen door and then turns to me, her expression cold and distant.

"I'm sorry about earlier. It's complicated, but thinking about it, maybe it is for the best. You're getting bigger, and working in a bar isn't a good idea. What if there's a fight or something?" I'm overtalking, and she looks more annoyed by the second. "I don't want the mother of my child—" She puts a hand up to stop me.

"One of the mothers to your children," she cuts in.

"Working behind a bar. It isn't safe," I continue, ignoring her little dig. "If you need money, I can sort that."

She laughs at my offer, shaking her head. "Get out," she orders.

"Don't be like this. We still have to talk about what's gonna happen. I'll set up a payment to go direct to your account each month. You're right about having a schedule set up. It makes sense to know where we all stand. I'm gonna be unavailable for the next few weeks or so, but if there're any problems, I'll allow Marshall to be around to let me know what's happening."

"You'll *allow* him to be around," she repeats, scoffing. "I'll tell you exactly how this is going to work, Kain Morgan. This is *my* baby, and with or without your consent, Marshall is in my life. I'll work for my money elsewhere, and from now on, you have no say . . . in *any* of it. Go take care of Ginger and leave me the hell alone," she hisses.

It's a shit move, but right now, I have no choice. I must put Ginger first, and if that means Harper will hate me for now, then it's how it has to be. I move towards her, and she backs up until she hits the table and has nowhere else to go. Leaning close, I breathe in her vanilla scent. I place a gentle kiss against her soft pink lips, and when her eyelids flutter closed, I take the kiss deeper. I commit this moment to memory and then take a step back, ignoring the tears that gather in her eyes. She can feel that this is goodbye. We both can. My baby will be safe with Harper, but I can't say the same about Ginger, so she has to be the priority. Harper can take this away thinking she's made the final decision, that she's being the strong one by pushing me away.

I leave without saying another word . . . before I change my mind.

Harper

I cry, and it's the ugly type of crying that you'd rather do alone, but Marshall insists on staying. He lets me sob against his shoulder and doesn't even complain when his T-shirt gets all wet. I wish I could fall in love with him—he's easy to love and my life would be simpler. Instead, I love that piece of shit who's walked away like he doesn't give a fuck about me or his baby.

"Yah know, you could always do some bar work for me," suggests Marshall. He recently opened a place in town called Legz, a strip bar with added extras.

I laugh, pushing myself to sit and wiping my face on the sleeves of my jumper. "You think people want to see me dance in this state?"

He laughs too and takes my hand in his, concentrating on my fingers. "Well, actually, you'd be surprised what people pay to see, but no, I meant behind the bar."

"You're creating a job because you want to help, and that's really sweet, but I'll sort something out," I say. I love that he wants to help me, which is another reason I should be madly in love with him.

"Seriously, I need a hand. Milly and Lacey are great, but they don't have experience like you do," he says, referring to two of the club girls who hang around the Hammers MC. Most people refer to them as the club whores, but I hate that. They want a better life, and they want it with a man they know will take care of them. Maybe they don't always go about it the right way, but sometimes, I feel for the girls and the shitty upbringings they've had.

"You think Kain will be happy about that?" I ask with a small laugh. There's no way he will want Marshall jumping to my rescue again.

"I don't care. That prick is stupid for treating you the way he does. He's chosen Ginger, it's time he lets you go now." The words sting. It's the truth, but it hurts so bad. I find myself nodding because I do need a job. I only have enough savings to carry me through for a month or two, then the baby is due and lord only knows what I'm going to do then.

"Okay, if you're sure. If customers want me to dance, can I oblige?" I joke, rubbing my bump seductively.

Marshall's face turns darker and he shakes his head. "Don't even think about it. You think Kain's possessive, then you haven't seen shit." I chew on my lower lip because that was hot. I get up and offer him a drink, mainly because I need to put distance between us before I jump on him. We do not need me to confuse the situation just because my hormones are going all crazy.

The next day, Marshall shows me around his new bar. It isn't anything like I pictured. I'd imagined dark red velvet and low lights, but it's modern. There's lots of glass and crystal, a white bar, and low-hanging chandeliers. Marshall had to get the backing of the club for the bar because it's on their territory, and naturally, the rules are that the brothers don't pay for drinks or dances.

Marshall reinforces to Milly and Lacey that they are not to tell Ginger or Kain that I'm helping out there or they'll be fired. They both seem fine with that, and we set about stocking the fridges and chatting about the clientele before opening. It feels nice to chat with the girls when usually I only have Sam or one of the guys to amuse me. Milly occupies us with tales of crazy guys when she's been on stage dancing, making us laugh. It feels like ages since I laughed.

The bar opens at ten in the evening. My feet hurt already, but I have to do this, and I remind myself of the money to come my way. The girls split all bar tips between bar staff, and by the looks of the suit-clad men walking in, there'll be lots of tipping.

I flirt my arse off, and being the newbie, I'm getting a lot of attention. I've had numerous requests for a dance which I've politely declined, mainly because Marshall is sitting at the end of the bar doing his books, though I know he's watching my every move. It's sweet and I'm reminded of a time when Kain cared enough to act like that.

By the end of the shift, I'm practically dead on my feet, but as the girls split the tip jar and I'm handed three hundred in notes, I do a little happy dance. This never happened at the clubhouse bar and I begin to think that everything so far has happened for a reason and that this job was meant to be.

The days roll into one. I work every hour that Marshall offers me, knowing there will come a time in a matter of weeks when I won't be able to stay on my feet and work so hard. I'm a week away from turning eight months and my bump suddenly feels so much lower and heavier than before. Giving myself a onceover in the mirror, my tight-fitted long dress shows off the huge bump, but luckily, it just about hides my swollen ankles.

Marshall is picking me up in ten minutes because Mila and Cooper are due home today and there's a gathering at the clubhouse. It's been almost two weeks since I saw Kain, but I'm told by Marshall that he's still around, albeit not himself. Ginger is due to give birth any day now, so I imagine he's distracted.

Stepping into the clubhouse bar is nerve-racking, and I take Marshall's hand for comfort. He happily obliges, giving it a gentle reassuring squeeze. Brook is the first to rush towards me and wrap me in a hug. "I'm so sorry I haven't been over to see you, but Asher is quite the handful," she says with a smile. Asher, Cooper's nephew, lives with Mila and Cooper, and because he has no parents, they're currently going through the adoption process to make everything official. Cooper doesn't want to risk Asher's father turning up and trying to take him because Asher's never known him.

"It's fine. I've nothing to tell anyway, my life is boring lately," I say with a nod towards my bump. She places her hands over it gently, adoration in her eyes. She and Tanner don't have children, though I can't understand why. Tanner is crazy in love with her and hardly ever leaves her side because he's obsessed with her, according to Mila, and Brook makes no secret of the fact that she loves kids and would love to have one of her own.

"How's Tanner coped with having Asher around?" I ask. Brook laughs, throwing a loving glance back towards her other half, who is watching us from his seat by the bar while Asher plays by his feet with some toy cars.

"It's driven him crazy. We've not had," she pauses and then lowers her voice, like she's conspiring, "sex." She giggles. "Two weeks of no sex is killing him, trust me. He literally bounced out of bed this morning with happiness because Cooper is back today. He doesn't like to share my attention."

I smile, feeling envious of her relationship. Maybe that's why they haven't had kids of their own, I muse. My skin prickles and I rub my arms while glancing around the packed-out bar. I know he's here somewhere, I can feel it.

"So, I need to hear what's going on with you and Kain," Brook pushes.

I shrug my shoulders. "Nothing. He's stepped away, and I'm getting on with life," I say, looking towards where Marshall is standing chatting to Woody, the club's Enforcer.

Brook follows my line of sight and her eyes widen. "Oh my god, have you and Marshall finally gotten together?" She almost squeals, and I look around anxiously while shushing her.

"No, nothing like that. He's become a really good friend. He's looking after me."

"And nothing's happened?" she queries, raising an eyebrow sceptically.

"No, I promised Kain I'd stay away from his brothers, and I will. We're friends."

Brook nods, but the smirk remains on her lips. "In other news, Kain is miserable," she says, her gossip mask clearly in place. "You should see the state of him. I don't know if he's out fighting every night or he's keeping a tiger in the office, but his face is a mess. Tanner reckons he's cage fighting to control his rage, but I'm not convinced."

My heart picks up pace, as it always does when talking about him. "Why doesn't Tanner just ask him?"

"You know what these men are like, all emotionless and hard-faced. He won't pry. Maybe now Cooper is coming back, things will improve. It could just be the pressure of managing the club."

There's a loud whistle and everyone quiets down. The door opens and Cooper enters followed by Mila, then cheers fill the room as the guys celebrate the return of their President. Asher is wrapped up between the two in a joint hug. He missed them badly. It's been just over two weeks, but it feels so much longer, and I make my way through the sea of large bodies until I reach Mila. She smiles widely at me before passing Asher to Cooper and wrapping me in her arms. I feel all my emotions bubble over and I burst into tears.

She keeps my head on her shoulder and shushes me soothingly. "Hey, I haven't been gone that long," she whispers. I feel myself being guided farther into the bar and then through the door of the clubhouse and into the main room, where she stops and pulls back to look at me. "Harps, what's wrong?" she asks, her face laced with concern.

"I'm so sorry. I don't know where that came from. It's just my hormones. How was the honeymoon? You look so tan," I observe, wiping my eyes and taking in Mila's golden skin. She's relaxed and glowing.

"Never mind me, what the hell is going on, Harper? You never cry, so I know something's wrong."

"It's just been a crazy two weeks. I'll tell you everything, but not right now when you've just walked in the door."

The clubhouse door opens and Cooper pops his head in. "Wife," he bellows, and Mila rolls her eyes, laughing.

"He thinks it's funny to address me like he's a caveman," she explains, and I smile. Cooper steps closer, and when he sees my tears, he frowns. "She's okay," Mila assures him. "She's promised to tell me all once I'm settled."

"Don't let that shit with Kain bother you. From what I hear, you're better off at Legz anyway," says Cooper, squeezing my shoulder gently. I shouldn't be surprised that he knows everything.

Mila looks between us, confusion marring her worried face. "You're working at Legz?" she asks.

"Temporarily, just until I can't stand anymore. I'm on the bar, not stripping," I clarify.

"Why? What happened to your job here?" I glance at Cooper, who winces and then waits for me to explain.

"Well, Kain and Ginger kind of asked me to leave," I say cautiously. Mila's expression morphs into anger and she balls her fists by her side.

She turns to Cooper for an explanation, and he shrugs his large shoulders. "Exactly what she said," he confirms, nodding in my direction.

Mila stomps from the room and towards the bar. I go to stop her, but Cooper takes my arm and shakes his head, a smirk playing on his lips. "Nah, let her get it out her system. Besides, I've been waiting for this moment since Irish called to tell me." Irish . . . of course, he'd spill all to Cooper. He's a prospect and is close to getting patched-in.

We go into the bar and find Mila is already in full swing, her finger pointed in Kain's face. "You make me fucking sick. You don't deserve her," she screams. Kain keeps his eyes fixed on his whiskey glass while Mila releases her angry words. Ginger is nowhere to be seen, and I'm thankful for that. "I gave you time to tell Ginger and you didn't, so I'm going to," she yells and turns away from him.

Kain is up off his chair in a split second and has hold of her wrist, halting her mid-step. All hell breaks loose as Cooper runs towards the pair, followed by some of the other brothers. Kain is up against the bar with Cooper holding him by the throat in seconds of him laying a hand on Mila.

"Don't ever put your hands on my ol' lady again!" Cooper's booming voice rattles off the walls. The other brothers step back, letting their President deal with Kain, but they remain close enough for instruction. I take in the bruises and scratches that already mar Kain's perfect face and I wonder what the hell's going on with him. I watch as Cooper drags him back into the clubhouse, slamming the door behind them.

Mila points to a bar stool, indicating for me to sit, which I do because she still looks crazy mad. Brook takes one beside me, and Mila takes the other. "Talk," orders Mila.

Brook laughs. "Wow. You've been married two weeks and you already sound like him," she points out.

Mila smiles cheekily and then gives me a pointed look. "Talk."

"I get it. Ginger struggles to have me around because . . ." I trail off, realising I don't know exactly why. Kain's had sex with numerous club girls and she doesn't struggle with any of them.

"Because he loves you and she can see it," continues Brook, and I roll my eyes. "You know I'm right. He can't take his eyes from you when you're in the same room, and she sees it like we all do, but for some reason, she's got a hold on Kain and he daren't leave her."

"Oh, wise one, aren't you so full of truths," I mock.

"She's got a point, Harp. Until she came back, you guys were hitting it off, so what changed?" asks Mila thoughtfully.

"She came back," I point out. "He loves Ginger. I appreciate you girls backing me, but you have to stop giving me false hopes. He doesn't love me. I'm just the girl he got pregnant on the side, and he regrets it and I think he feels guilty. But he loves her, and they're going to be an amazing little family. I have to step away now because she's won. She won him, and I have to bow out gracefully."

As I say the words, they hit me hard. Every word is truth, and although I've thought it over and over, it's the first time I've voiced it to anyone. The realisation that Kain isn't mine and never was hurts all over again. I pursued him relentlessly, playing games, making him jealous, and even after Ginger came back, I didn't step back. I chased him, knowing he had a girlfriend. I've become the type of person I hate.

I've become just like my father.

CHAPTER SIX

Kain

I wiggle my jaw from side to side. The punch that Cooper landed felt like he'd broken it, but thankfully, I can move it. I feel my eye swelling by the second as Cooper glowers down at me. He knows I won't hit him back. I deserve every hit because I did the unthinkable—I grabbed the arm of his pregnant wife. I don't know what I was thinking. I heard Mila say those words, that she was going to tell Ginger about Harper's baby, and I panicked. I'm not sure how Ginger would take that news right now. She isn't stable enough, and I had to protect my woman too.

"You know how much it hurts me to do that to you, my best friend, my VP?" yells Cooper, pacing angrily.

"I fucked up, brother. I'm sorry," I mutter.

"What the hell's going on, Kain? I don't even know you right now."

"Stress is all. Ginger's about ready to drop this kid, but I'm not ready, and then in another month, Harper's gonna have my secret kid.

My life is a mess," I admit. Cooper smacks me around the head again, a look of disgust on his face.

"You think you can sit in here being all self-pitying and shit? Man the fuck up. You brought your private life here and it spilled out into my club and caused chaos. Get a grip on it."

"It won't happen again, Coop," I say.

"No damn right it won't. Maybe you need a break. I can ask Marshall to take on VP while you sort your shit out," he suggests, and I practically jump from my seat.

"No," I yell, and he glares at me, pure rage on his face. I take a deep breath and continue, much calmer. "I mean, please, Pres, don't do that. I'll sort myself out. I can handle it. I'll talk to Ginger and Harper and make it right." He looks doubtful, but there is no way that fucker is taking my VP badge. First, he gets Harper, and then he gets my badge—not happening.

"You realise all you're doing is pushing Harper towards him, don't you? I don't get what's going on. Why Ginger when you love Harper?" It isn't the first time he's asked the question, and it won't be the first time I've had to lie my way out of answering with the truth.

"I love Ginger, and we have history." I sigh.

Cooper leans in close, his expression full of disappointment. "Get the fuck out of my office. The audacity to sit here and lie to my face. Of all the people . . . *me*?"

"It's the truth," I lie.

"Do you want me to finish the job, Kain? Because if you sit here and lie to my face once more, I'm gonna end the only guy I've ever respected enough to keep around. Get out of here and come back to me when you've got your shit together. Marshall is stepping up." We glare at each other, neither willing to back down. I ball my fists, and he smirks. "I dare you," he goads. It's a decision he won't change. I know him too well, and me picking a fight with my President will only earn me a stay in the hospital.

I storm out of the office, slamming the door hard enough for the small glass window to shatter. "You're paying for that!" I hear him yell after me.

Heading out to my bike, I throw my leg over it and rev the engine to life. Harper runs from the bar and stops at my side. "What happened?" she pants.

"Go back inside," I growl.

"No. Talk to me, Kain," she begs.

"I can't," I grit out. She throws her leg over the bike behind me and wraps her arms around my waist.

"Then ride," she says, squeezing my waist tight. I close my eyes, allowing her arms to bring me comfort. I've missed them more than I've realised. I wait while she takes the spare helmet from the top box and quickly fastens it. Her arms slide back into place, and I speed from the car park before anyone sees us.

I know she must be uncomfortable on the bike being so heavily pregnant, but I ride for half an hour before taking a turn off the road and into the woods. Sam has a cabin up here, where the guys go when they need time away.

I stop the bike and hold it steady as she carefully climbs off, grimacing as she straightens her back. I take her by the hand and pull her towards the log cabin. Finding the key in the usual hiding spot, I open the door, but before she's stepped inside fully, I have her against me and I'm kissing her hard and hungry. I'm outta control, I can feel that I am. Harper is trying to pull away, but I keep on kissing her, pressing my mouth over hers and forcing my tongue between her lips. Her fists pound against my chest, forcing my senses to return. I pull away panting and turn my back to her, so she can't see the shame I feel.

"Christ, Kain, what's wrong with you?" she asks, moving into my line of sight.

"Is it not as gentle as Marshall's kiss?" I sneer, and she sighs. "You don't like the beast in me because it's not all romance and flowers like it is with him," I continue. "You used to like the way I took control," I add, moving closer to her and running my finger along her collar bone. She folds her arms over her chest and lowers her eyes to the ground.

"This isn't like you, Kain. Talk to me." I hate the sympathetic tone in her voice, the way she begs me with those pretty blues of hers. Anger is bubbling inside, and she notices the way my fists curl. She takes a step back and that pisses me off more. Twice now, she's looked at me with fear when I've never hit her and I never would.

"I don't want to talk, Harper. I want to fuck. It's what we do, isn't it? You're always there when I need a release," I snarl. "That's why you came running out after me, like the fucking guardian angel of the big bad biker. Does it make you feel better knowing you can calm the beast inside me just with your damn sweet pussy?" I growl, and she backs away farther. I'm in her space and I didn't even realise I'd moved. "So, come on, Harper, do what you're good at and fuck me."

Her eyes look to the floor, hurt evident in the way she holds herself. I can't help it, I'm mad as hell, and before I can rein it in, I'm back in her face. "You know, if you hadn't fucking seduced me in the first place, none of this would have happened. I'd be happy, Ginger would be happy, and my life wouldn't be so fucked up," I hiss with a viciousness in my tone I only use when I'm torturing an enemy.

Harper swipes at a stray tear as it runs down her flushed cheek. She takes a deep breath and then I see the change in her eyes as she fixes me with a steely glare. "Take me home," she says firmly.

"You got on the bike thinking you could save me. Did you think we were gonna have a cup of tea and a good old chat?" I ask in my poshest tone. "That's not the life you signed up for when you fucked me and decided to keep my kid. You like this, the arguing, the angry fucking . . . it's what you wanted. It's why you pursued me in the first place."

"No, it isn't. I saw it for what it was, a good time. I liked you, and let's not pretend that you weren't fully invested in what I had to offer, Kain. Not once did you mention Ginger when I was sucking your cock. We had great sex, but that's all we had, and I see that now. But as we're going to have a child together, I thought the least I owed you was an ear to listen, to check that you're okay, because clearly you have shit going on that's tearing you up. But I'll be damned if I'm going to stand here and be your punching bag." She pulls her mobile phone from her pocket.

"What are you doing?"

"I'm calling someone to come and get me." I hit the phone out of her hand without thinking, and it falls to the floor, breaking apart and scattering in different directions. She moves farther away from me, and the cautiousness returns to her eyes.

"Stop looking at me like you're scared. I've not once laid a finger on you that you've not wanted me to. I've never fucking hurt you," I snap.

She scoffs. "Not physically, no."

I sigh heavily. "Your man's the new Vice President," I mutter, dropping down on the couch. I watch her confusion form before the news sinks in and she realises what I'm saying. "The Pres isn't happy with my recent behaviour. I think firing you was bad enough but grabbing Mila like that was the final nail in my coffin." She sits on the couch opposite me, resting her hands on her stomach. I follow the movement with my eyes. I've not been to any of the classes, any of the scans, and I've not even heard the heartbeat of the unborn child that she carries for me.

"That must sting," she says, absentmindedly rubbing circles over her bump.

"It stings knowing that he's taken my role in the club as well as with my woman," I confess.

She sighs. "He didn't take your woman. Ginger is still at home waiting for you."

"You know I didn't mean her," I mutter.

"Don't, Kain." Her eyes plead with me.

"He's stepping into the life I should have had," I continue.

She shakes her head. "You have the life you should have had, with Ginger. I have the life I should have had on my own with my baby," she says, and my heart cracks a little more. "There is no me and Marshall. Christ, I wish there were. I want to love him because he's amazing. He treats me so well, and it doesn't faze him that I'm pregnant with another man's baby. He's ready to take on all that shit and lose a brother over it. I should be in love with him, but I'm not, and I think he sticks around hoping that it'll change. And who knows, maybe one day, when I finally wake up and realise you won't ever love me like you do her, that's when I'll concentrate on myself. Until then, I don't have a choice," she almost whispers. "My mother always said I'd end up like this because I always wanted the men who didn't want me."

I want to tell her that it isn't true, that if I had the choice, it would be her every time. Instead, I sit quietly, watching her hand circle that bump over and over.

"You should go for it," I mutter, and she looks up at me. "You should try with Marshall," I clarify. It breaks my heart to say it, and by the look on her face, it hurts her too. "He'd take care of you and the baby." I move over to her couch and place my palm gently over the bump, unable to control the urge to feel my child inside of her. My huge hand just about covers it, and I smile at how petite Harper is compared to me. I inhale sharply when I feel the hard kick under her skin. "What a kick," I say with a smile.

"It would be easier to love Marshall." She looks lost in thought, and I wonder if she's picturing him right now. "But I can't lead him on. He's too good for that." I nod in understanding. She doesn't want to be involved in any more drama.

"If I stepped away, moved away," I say, "would it make it easier for you?"

"No, I don't want that. I've ruined your life enough, the last thing I want is to live with the fact that you've moved away from your brothers."

"I could transfer to another chapter. Maybe it will be good for me and Ginger."

"Kain, something tells me that you'll be needing Cooper and your brothers over the next few months. I can see things aren't good, the bruises, the scratches. I don't want to make assumptions but . . ." She trails off, and I feel a lump rise in my throat.

I don't cry. I haven't cried since I was maybe three years old. I turn away from her slightly so that she doesn't see, but she places her hand on my back and gently rubs circles like she did over her bump. A wetness covers my cheeks, and for once, it isn't blood. I feel Harper shift and then she's pressed against my back, her arms hung loosely around my neck and her face pressed against my shoulder.

CHAPTER SEVEN

Harper

I've never seen this kind of emotion from Kain, or from any of the guys in the MC. When they're upset, they break shit, but they don't ever break down. I stay wrapped around him, his shoulders gently shaking in my hold as he releases whatever's been building these last few months. I don't speak, don't try to look at him, just hold him, because I don't think either of us know the protocol in this situation. It's a first for us.

I wait until his shoulders still, then I sit back against the couch and gently tug him to lay down. He places his head in my lap, facing away from me. I remove the tie from his man-bun and begin to run my fingers through his dark hair, gently twisting it the way he likes. Eventually his breathing evens out and he falls into a deep sleep.

I run my fingers up and down his bare arm, over the tattoos covering his skin. He's added more over the last few months, and my fingers stop on the harp that hides amongst the various tattoos forming his sleeve. A harp. He'd joked that my name was well suited because I played him like a harp, though I tried to tell him that the saying was 'play him like a fiddle'. My fingers dance over the tattoo as I wonder if Ginger has noticed it or realised it's for me.

I'm not sure how long I sit with him sleeping in my lap. My backside is numb and it's dark outside, but he looks so peaceful that I daren't wake him. But eventually, I slide gently along the couch until I'm free. I lower his head onto the cushion and breathe a sigh of relief when he settles in and remains asleep.

I move quietly around the beautiful cabin. I find some Lucky Charms cereal in the cupboard and it's still in date, which means Sam must have been here recently. He loves Lucky Charms. I shovel some into my mouth, I'm so hungry. Picking up the pieces of my mobile phone, I slot the battery back into place and find I have text messages from Mila and Marshall. I reply to both saying that I'm fine and not to worry. There's no way I'm waking Kain to take me home. It's getting late, and he'll probably sleep the night through now. He needs the rest.

I pull some fresh blankets from a cupboard in the bedroom and make up the double bed. Then, I take a cool shower to freshen up before climbing into bed. It's surprisingly comfy, and I feel myself drifting off to sleep as soon as I snuggle down.

Sometime later, I stir, inhaling a shaky breath. There's a pleasure building, and I'm somewhere between sleep and wake. I stretch out and open one eye. Kain is spooning me from behind and his hand is up my top, cupping my breast as his thumb and finger massage my erect nipple. I sigh, because it's been too long since I've had an orgasm that wasn't the result of my rubbery vibrating friend. His other hand is dangerously close to my panties, running up and down my thigh.

"What are you doing?"

"One last time. I'll let you go, I promise, but just give me one last time," he whispers, kissing my neck gently. His hand brushes across the thin material of my underwear. A moan slips from my lips as a shot of pleasure hits my core. When I don't protest, he moves his fingers under the scrap of lace and brushes over my swollen clit. Rolling me gently onto my back, he settles himself over me, his weight resting on his elbows. Slowly, he lowers his lips to mine. The kiss is soft and slow, different from all the other times. He begins to move down my body, kissing and licking until he settles between my legs, nipping at my inner thighs. He pulls at my panties, shredding the material in his hands, leaving me bare to him. Pushing my legs farther apart, he runs his tongue along my slick opening, humming in approval. I wriggle, but he holds me firm as he assaults my pussy with his mouth, and as I feel the build-up, I begin to pant. He pushes a finger into my opening, and I groan out loud as the waves crash through me, my body shuddering uncontrollably.

I lay staring up at the ceiling as my body reduces to mush and my breath comes in short bursts. Kain crawls up my body, lining himself at my opening. He rubs against my wetness a few times, and I jerk against him at the sensitivity of my clit. I place my hands on his shoulders as he inches in gradually, closing his eyes in pleasure. My hands run over the faint bruises and marks on his chest, and there're so many. I trail over a half- healed cut that's red and raised. It must have been deep before it began healing.

He takes my hand, gently guiding it away while shaking his head. He brings my fingers to his lips and sucks them into his mouth, all the time moving gently in and out. He sits back on his heels and grips my thighs hard, thrusting faster, chasing his release. I feel his cock swell, and he groans out loud, shuddering. Then, he stills, his eyes closed, his head thrown back in pleasure as he releases inside me. I love him like this, vulnerable and unguarded.

He stays sat back on his heels, his chest heaving with the exertion. He slips out of me, his cock now semi-hard, and he looks down to where we were connected. "Was I too rough?" he asks quietly, keeping my legs apart while he watches his fluids run from me. I shake my head. He reaches over to a box of tissues on the bedside table and wipes me carefully. It's the first time Kain's ever been gentle, and it makes my heart swell.

He settles down behind me again, spooning me. Tears leak silently from my eyes, and I'm not sure whether I'm happy or sad. All I know is that whenever Kain is around, I always end up crying.

Kain

I watch the rise and fall of Harper's naked chest. She's gorgeous, inside and out. Every curve, every dimple, it just adds to her beauty. The thought of her feeding my child warms me, and it's a sight I hope I get to see. Last night, I cried, and Harper didn't judge me. She didn't laugh, she didn't quiz me or hit out at me . . . she just held me. Her strength amazes me, and I know without a doubt she'd have made a perfect ol' lady.

My cock stirs to life, and I close my eyes, resting my head against the headboard as I stroke my hand lazily up and down my shaft.

I feel her shift beside me, but I keep my eyes closed. Her hands take hold of my shoulders, and I feel her straddle me. She grips my length in her tiny hand and lines the head up with her entrance. Running her hands over my cheeks and into my hair, she pulls my face up to look at her. Her perfect lips are slightly open as she pushes herself down onto my erection, all the while looking into my eyes. We don't use words to communicate how we feel right now, and as she brings herself to orgasm, I kiss her, taking her breath as she cries out in pleasure, the sounds muffled.

Her orgasm drips down my cock, driving me wild. I hold her hips and thrust up in a frenzied moment of want. She lets me take what I need, and when I'm close to coming, she begins to move against me, taking my hands and holding them above my head. I feel my orgasm rushing to the forefront, and as I yell out, she keeps the pace exactly the same, drawing out every ounce of pleasure I feel.

My breaths continue to escape in short, sharp heaves when she lifts from me and stands. She disappears into the bathroom, and I hear the shower turn on. When she returns ten minutes later, she's dressed, and she's used my hair tie to pile her locks onto her head in a messy bun.

"Where are you going?" I ask, confused.

She lowers to the edge of the bed and takes my hand in hers. "I texted Mila asking her to come and get me. She won't tell anyone—I've sworn her to secrecy." My heart hammers in my chest. I know what's coming and I'm not ready for it.

"Why? Stay, at least for today," I say, and she smiles sadly. I'm not ready to go back to Ginger and all the problems that we face. I like being wrapped up in a bubble with Harper, where I can pretend my life is good.

"I'm glad we talked, Kain. I think we can move forward now, and we're in a much better place. Let's walk away from here happier and go back to our lives. Your baby is due any time now, so you need to focus on Ginger and your family. If you need me for anything, you're always welcome in my home, even if you just need shelter from the storm," she says with a smile.

I slide my hands under my thighs to stop me grabbing hold of her and keeping her with me. Harper stands and leans down to place a kiss on my cheek. I close my eyes, and when I open them, she's gone.

I stay in this same position for over an hour, contemplating my life and the fuck-ups I've made. Blaming Harper for pursuing me was harsh, I wanted her to chase me. I wanted her to want me, and every time I rejected her, it was knowing that she'd come back for more because she wanted me, and she was a determined little firecracker. When Ginger returned, I had a moment of weakness, and in some ways, I used her to make Harper jealous. It's what we did back then to get each other's attention. I remember back to when Cooper hired her as a bartender. He said she'd have me weak at the knees and begging for pussy before the first month was out, and he was right. Harper was exactly my type, and playing hard to get with her was the hardest game I've ever had to play.

I check my mobile, pretty sure Ginger would have called me a thousand times, but there are no missed calls, which alarms me slightly. Maybe Cooper covered my arse and told her I was on a run. I get dressed and decide the first person I need to see is Cooper because he deserves an apology. I look at my face in the mirror. My eye is closed from the swelling and the other is bruised to fuck.

The clubhouse bar is empty with just Sam sitting behind it. "Hey, is the Pres about?" I ask, and Sam nods and points to the clubhouse door. I go through and find Cooper in the office with his door open. He looks up when he hears the thudding of my boots. We stare at each other for a few silent seconds and then he points to the chair positioned in front of his desk.

"Where'd yah go?" he asks.

"Sam's place, the cabin," I mutter. "Listen, Coop, I'm sorry about yesterday. I'm sorry about everything that's happened these last few months. I'm fucking shit up left, right, and centre, and I just need you to know I'm sorry."

Cooper eyes me before nodding in acceptance. "It tears me up to see you like this, Kain. We're more than just brothers, and I thought you'd come and talk to me." He sighs. I've known Cooper since forever and don't really remember a time when he wasn't in my life.

"How did you choose between them?" I blurt out. "Between Anna and Mila?" Cooper sighs at the mention of Anna's name. He thought she'd died, and he was broken, but then she turned up right before his first wedding to Mila and it almost ruined them.

"I had no choice. Anna had a gun pointed at Mila and my heart chose for me. Sometimes you don't know what the right choice is until you're forced to make a decision." Cooper shot Anna dead. I shudder, hoping I never have to make that choice because I know Harper would win every time and fuck knows what that would do to Ginger.

"Ginger is sick, in here," I say, tapping my head, and Cooper raises his eyebrows in surprise. "She can't take her pills at the moment, so she's a little crazy sometimes. I can't leave her like that, so I'm asking you for some understanding and support to help me through this.

When she's given birth, things might be better, but until then, I need my brothers around me," I say. Cooper stands, and I do the same, then he pulls me into a hug, slapping me on the back.

"It's all I wanted to hear, brother. The truth," he says. "And what about Harper?"

"Me and Harper are good. We talked and we've agreed this is how it's gotta be. We're taking a step back from each other," I say.

"So, does that mean you're giving Marshall the green light?" presses Cooper, going into his desk and pulling out a bottle of whiskey. He places two glasses on the desk and pours into each.

"I'll step away, but I don't need to give him the green light because that's up to her. She says she doesn't feel like that about him, but who knows, maybe when I'm out of the picture, things will change," I say with a shrug.

"Shit, I never thought I'd hear you say that." Cooper hands me a glass. "You're seriously letting her go? What about the kid?"

"That too. Maybe at some point in the future, but right now, I need to be with Ginger and the baby, and she can't cope with me running off to Harper." I feel like a weight has been lifted as I drink the whiskey back and wince. One night with Harper and my head's already clearer. I'm not sure where that'll leave me when she isn't around anymore, and I get in a mess again.

CHAPTER EIGHT

Harper

"You seem chirpy," says Gloria. I'm singing as I wipe the dishes. It isn't often I see Gloria twice in one week, but I'm trying to keep my father sweet. I managed to avoid dinner with him and Mum for another two days. I have that amount of time to find a man in a suit who thinks I'm not crazy and will pretend to be madly in love with me so we can convince them that there is a father for this baby.

Anton stands nearby, topless in denim cut-off, and he's rubbing his hair with a towel. "Why are you here again?" he asks coldly.

"I came to see the twins. I got paid early from a client and I got them a teddy bear," I say brightly. The girls have wanted a talking teddy bear for weeks now, and I'm sick of not being able to treat them.

"Doesn't the missing sperm donor earn plenty of money, or do you have to wait for payments to be settled from your clients?" he sneers.

"Anton," sighs Gloria, "stop with the jibes." She leaves the kitchen to tend to the twins who are now squabbling.

"Well, doesn't he?" he asks, moving closer.

"It's none of your business," I snap. He's ruining my good mood. I feel his hip brush against mine as he reaches for a glass, and I move away quickly. He goes through stages of being weird like this. It makes me uncomfortable, and I think he gets off on that.

"Your deadbeat father was out all-night last night," he says.

"Gloria said he had a meeting that ran late," I say with a shrug. Of course, I know the truth, but I always keep up with the lies.

"We both know that was code for cheating," he says. "One day, I'll catch the slimy bastard out and I'll take great pleasure in bringing his world crashing down just like he did to my father." I roll my eyes. I've heard the threat so many times now, but my father is the greatest liar going, which is how my mother is fooled day in and day out. I used to wait when I was young and more naïve for her to tell me she'd caught him, and she was leaving him. Every time they argued, I held my breath, hoping it was because she'd uncovered the truth and I wouldn't have to lie anymore, but she never did, and his lie became mine. "I'm going to take you both down. Maybe I'll drag yours out while your father watches. I'd like to see if he comes undone when he sees his precious little girl ruined."

I step back, avoiding his hand as he reaches to move the strap of my dress. "What the hell are you talking about?" I snap. "You think my father gives a crap about me?" I laugh. "He's only ever interested in himself. I thought you were observant."

Gloria comes back into the room as Anton leaves, and I go back to wiping the dishes. Gloria eyes me suspiciously. "Everything okay?" I nod, forcing a smile.

I get home and send a text off to Mila and Brook. "I need a man, just on loan. He needs to have no visible tattoos and needs to dress well, speak well, and be able to lie."

Brook sends a laughing emoji, and Mila calls me. I answer, and she adds Brook into the call. "Spill the beans," she orders, and I explain that I've not told my parents about Kain. Mila knows how pompous my parents can be, and she also knows the trauma I go through with my father, so she gets why I don't need the extra stress. "Have you asked Marshall?" she suggests,

"No, I don't want to confuse things between us."

"I'd loan Tanner out, but he won't leave my side since I handed Asher back over. I only leave the bedroom to eat, drink, and pee," says Brook.

"Where is he now?" I ask with a laugh, imagining he isn't too far from her.

"Next to me." She sighs, and we all laugh.

"Well, the only gentleman I can think of is Sam and he's way too old. What's their views on age gap relationships?" jokes Mila.

"Come on, guys, I need your help. There must be someone we know."

"I can ask Cooper," suggests Mila. "He always knows the answer." We groan and make puking noises down the phone at her, and she laughs. "I'm going now. I'll text you if he can think of anyone."

Mila later sent me a text saying Cooper had sorted it and all I needed to do was be ready on time and he'd send a suited man to pick me up in a flashy car. That suited man stands before me now, looking sheepish.

"Marshall, I'm sorry about this. I didn't realise Cooper would rope you in."

"You could have asked me yourself," he says. I pick my handbag up and check I have everything I need.

"I didn't want to confuse things. We're good as friends, and us making up some lie to my family about a relationship is blurring the lines."

"Exactly, we're mates, you can ask me stuff like this and I'm happy to help. One question—why didn't you just tell them you were single?"

"Because, well, it's complicated." I sigh. "Marshall, it's so important that you stick to the story."

Marshall rolls his eyes. "Yeah, yeah, I'm rich, blah, blah." He's laughing, and it pisses me off. This is serious and exactly the reason I needed a real stand-in.

"Marshall, listen to me," I say, gripping his arm. "My father is controlling and harsh and all kinds of messed up. Please don't fuck this up and make my life worse. If he lashes out . . ." I trail off and take a deep breath. "If he gets nasty, please don't stand up to him for me. It will make it worse for my mother."

Marshall's smile fades and concern crosses his face. "What do you mean by lashes out?"

"He just gets crazy sometimes, so promise me," I plead, and he rubs my arm reassuringly. I'm pretty sure my father wouldn't dare embarrass himself by being rude in front of a man he thinks is rich, but you never can tell with his mood swings.

"Whatever you want, Harps," he mutters.

Dinner is a strange affair. What began as them meeting me for lunch turned into an evening meal in a swanky restaurant. I shift uncomfortably. I hate these kinds of places, and the look on Marshall's face tells me he does too. My parents arrive, and we stand. I kiss my mum on the cheek and then my father. "This is Marshall," I introduce with a nervous smile. My father shakes Marshall's hand, and I can see Marshall gives a firm grip. I warned him about my father thinking that weak handshakes were a sign of a lesser man.

"It's so nice to finally meet you," gushes my mother, kissing Marshall on the cheek. I see the bruises on her wrist when her sleeve rides up her arm as she reaches for him, but she pulls it down quickly in a well-practised move. We all take our seats, and the waiter brings us the wine menu. My father looks across at Marshall.

"Maybe you'd like to order the wine. Harper tells me you're a businessman, so you must have a good taste for wine." I panic. Marshall would never drink wine, but he smiles calmly and looks over the menu.

"Personally, I don't drink it. I'm more of a whiskey man, but if I was to order, it would be . . ." He takes a moment and then smiles, looking up at the waiter. "The 1979 Chateau Prince Larquey." The waiter gives a nod before wandering off to retrieve a wine I've never heard of.

"Good choice," mutters my father, and I think he just about chokes on the words. "So, what is it that you actually do?"

"I custom build motorbikes. I also have a nightclub, which I'm hoping to expand eventually."

"Custom build bikes? So, you belong to the MC?" my father asks, glaring at me.

"No, sir, I just like building bikes," says Marshall simply.

"I love motorbikes." My mother sighs, and I frown in her direction. She says the weirdest stuff sometimes. "What do your parents do?" she asks.

"They're dead," he says with no emotion. I didn't know that, and I find myself looking at him. He smiles at me.

"You didn't tell me that."

He shrugs, keeping his face emotionless. "It never came up."

"So, you and my daughter are . . ." my father fishes for confirmation.

"Please, don't embarrass me," I mutter.

"It's fine." Marshall smiles. "We are in love, and we're having a baby. Apologies that it's taken me this long to introduce myself to you, but things have been busy."

"Harper uses that same excuse," mutters my father dryly. The waiter brings the wine and pours my father a glass to taste. He does so and then nods, a signal that he approves.

"Can I have two glasses of water for me and the lady," asks Marshall, and the waiter nods.

"Do you plan on marrying her?" my mother asks, and I groan.

"No," I snap. "I don't believe in marriage," I add, and she blushes.

My father scowls. "Your child will be a bastard," he says.

"My child will want for nothing, especially love. I don't need to be married to prove anything to anyone."

Marshall watches me. "You really don't believe in marriage?" he asks, and I shake my head. Why would I believe in that after watching my train wreck parents ruin each other all in the name of marriage?

"You don't seem to know a lot about each other. Have you even talked, or is it always fucking?" snaps my father, and I glance around to the other tables to see if he was overheard.

"Mainly fucking but the occasional chat," I hiss across the table, and my mother presses her lips together in a firm line. She hates arguing because it usually ends in fighting and screaming.

"Does he know how much you like doing that, Harper?" asks my father, and my mother gently places her hand over his to shush him.

"Sorry, Marshall, I can't do this." I sigh, standing, and my mother grips my hand, pleading me with her eyes. I take a deep breath and then lower back into my chair. My father gives me a satisfied smile. "My father is referring to my teenage years," I say coldly. "I wasn't always good at following his rules, was I, Daddy?" My father shifts anxiously, and it gives me great satisfaction to know I can make him sweat. It's my mother who will pay, though, and so I bite my lip, trying to gain control of myself. "Sorry, ignore me," I add with a small smile in Marshall's direction. He nods, but I know this will raise questions when we leave here.

We sit in silence for a few minutes until the waiter brings our water and then takes our food order. I pray hard that it comes super quick because I want to get out of here. Marshall makes small talk with my mother. She loves her garden, and he fakes an interest in it to keep her talking. I occasionally throw my father a dirty look before people-watching out the window.

64

After we've eaten, I follow my mother to the bathroom to 'powder our noses', something I've never done in my life but it's her code for a gossip. We're washing our hands when she looks at me through the mirror, pain in her eyes. "Why do you set him off like that?" she asks.

"Because I'm not like you. I can't let him tear me down and just take it," I snap.

"It's easier that way," she mutters, and I roll my eyes. I hate that she keeps quiet for an easy life. There have been times I've wanted her to flip the switch and give him just as good as she gets, but she never does.

"Sometimes it's a happier life when you just stand up for yourself. Try it."

"You never got it." She sighs. "It isn't as easy as just standing up to him."

I shake my head in annoyance and move for the door. "It is, Mum. It really is. You just have to want it."

After dinner, we drive home in silence. Marshall occasionally glances across at me, but when I remain staring straight ahead, he goes back to concentrating on the road. He stops the car outside my place, and I unfasten my belt. "Do you want me to come in?" he asks, and I shake my head.

"Thanks so much for that. I'm sorry it was shit," I say, and he laughs.

"If you ever need to talk, Harper, I'm here for you," he offers, and I smile gratefully.

CHAPTER NINE

Kain

It's been five days since I saw Harper. I've kept to my word and stayed away from her. It makes it easier that she no longer works for the club, not that Ginger would know because she hasn't left our house in days. She hasn't even moved from our bed for that exact amount of time. I don't even think she realised I was gone for a night, which was good news for me and meant I didn't have to explain and lie my way out of it. I open the curtains and then the window, and Ginger winces at the stream of light that hits her.

"Up," I say, but she ignores me. If she weren't pregnant, it would be easier to throw her over my shoulder. I rip the covers back from her, and she curls herself into a ball. I sigh. "You need a bath or a shower or something." Her eyes bore into me like she hates me, but she doesn't speak. "Fine, I'm going to just lift you up and take you because if you go into labour in this state, they'll lock your arse up again, and you don't want that," I say.

I slide my arms under her and lift her. She curls into me, which makes a change because I was fully expecting her to hit out. I carry her into the bathroom and gently put her down to stand, then I reach inside the shower, turn it on, and go about undressing her. The thought enters my mind that I could quite possibly end up doing this for the rest of our lives if she doesn't start to feel better after she gives birth.

Ginger came to the club when she was in her late teens. She'd hang around the garage and chat to the brothers while they worked. She'd do a shop run when they needed a drink or cigarettes. Thinking back, she was a little erratic even then.

I liked her from the moment I saw her. She was wild and lived life on the edge. She was the type to lean over the edge of a cliff and wave her hands in the air. We started hooking up, just the odd night here and there when I'd drink too much or club arse became too monotonous. After a year or so, she just disappeared. I didn't know much about her family and didn't have a contact number for her, so I got on with life. One day, she turned back up and we picked up where we left off. The same thing happened maybe six months later, and it kept happening.

I later found out that she was sectioned and that her mental health was poor after she'd been in a car accident as a teenager. She was left with a brain injury that affected her emotions, her rational thinking, her memory, and she often fell into bouts of depression and anxiety. She was medicated for bi-polar. The last time she returned, it was to tell me she was pregnant with my child and that she had to make a choice, either stop taking her medications or terminate the pregnancy. She chose the latter, and I promised I'd look after her. So far, I've been failing her.

Once she's in the shower, I take the sponge and squirt her favourite wash onto it. She watches my every move but she still won't speak. I wash her body and the baby kicks as I run the sponge over her large bump, and I smile. Ginger shows me nothing, and I wonder if she even felt it. I wash her hair and once we're done, I wrap her in a towel and take her back into the bedroom, where I sit her in front of her mirror and blow dry her hair.

"Why don't we go out and get some food?" I suggest. She makes eye contact via the mirror but doesn't speak. "Come on, baby, talk to me. I can't take this." I sigh.

"I hate you," she says coldly, and I nod. I know that, because she tells me often. "This is all your fault." I nod again, setting the hair dryer on the table and going to her drawers to find some clean clothes. I help her to stand and then crouch before her, holding some shorts for her to step into. "You hate me too," she says.

"I really don't hate you, Ginger." I sigh, pulling the clean T-shirt over her head. She slaps me hard, and I take her arm and guide it into the shirt. She slaps me again. On top of the wounds I already have from my argument with Cooper, the slap stings. I feel the cut under my eye split open again and blood trickles down my cheek. "Just say it. Say that you hate me," she yells.

"I don't hate you. Calm down, think of the baby."

"That's all you want me for is this damn baby. Have it, take it now," she screams, hitting her stomach.

"Don't do that," I hiss, taking her wrist. She uses her free hand to hit me again, catching my ear and then scratching at my neck. Once I have her other hand, I spin her away from me and hold her back to my front. She struggles, kicking back at my shins and catching me hard. "Fuck, Ginger, stop," I growl.

"Get it out of me," she screams. The neighbours will think I'm killing her, so I release her and step away. She turns to me, anger pouring from her. "Hit me back. Why don't you ever hit me back?" she yells.

"Because I love you. Because I know you can't help this." She laughs, an evil glint in her eye, and then she begins throwing things at me, anything within her reach. Perfume bottles shatter against the wall, a dinner plate still containing last night's dinner that she refused to eat breaks, and then I feel something crack against my skull and my vision blurs slightly. I back out of the room. I can't help her when she's like this, and me staying in there with her just infuriates her more. I rub the throbbing pain at the back of my head and see blood on my hand. I don't know what she threw at me, but, man, it hurt. I make my way down the stairs and let out a groan when I hear police sirens. The neighbours must have called the cops. I slip my feet into my boots and head out the back. Jumping the fence, I make my escape, heading straight for the clubhouse.

Tanner hands me a beer as Brook opens the first aid kit. "So, are you gonna tell us what happened?" she asks.

"Nope," I mutter. She presses something cold to my head, and I hiss. "Did you do that on purpose?"

"As if I would." She smirks, wiping at the cut.

Irish rushes into the room. "Cops wanting to talk to you, Kain," he whispers. "I didn't tell them you were here, just said I'd check and see if anyone knew where you were." Tanner stands, placing his beer on the table.

"I'll go and speak to them," he grunts, marching off.

"Did Ginger do this?" blurts out Brook.

"Nope," I say.

"Because if she did, it's okay to talk about it, Kain. I know you, and I know you wouldn't hurt her, but what she's doing to you is not okay." She sighs.

I stand, moving away from her to peek through the blinds at the cops. "Shut the fuck up, Brook. No woman is gonna get away with hitting me," I lie.

"I'm just saying, if she did, you can talk to me. I wouldn't tell anyone, not the guys, not the girls." I eye her for a second. Maybe talking to her might help, and maybe she'd know what to do, but before I can answer, the moment is broken by the cops pushing their way in.

"Kain Morgan?" asks the first. "We need to talk to you regarding an incident that was reported to us."

"So, talk," I snap coldly. The cop behind the first one speaks into his radio for back-up, which usually means they're gonna take me in. They take one look at my size and assume I'm gonna kick off, which is the exact reason I ran from Ginger's. They'll blame me for the fight.

"We had reports of a domestic incident at your home." He glances down at his notepad and then reads out the address.

"Well, as you can see, officer, I'm here, not there."

"We entered the property and found your partner, a Miss Virginia Shaw. She was quite badly shaken, and the bedroom was a mess," he says, his tone accusing.

"What's she say?" I ask, because I know she wouldn't have said it was me.

"At the moment, sir, she isn't talking. We have an officer with her at the hospital, but she's badly shaken, and neighbours reported seeing you leave the back entrance as police arrived."

"They've said it was me?" I ask, doubting anyone would name me. "They gave my name?"

The officer smirks. "I think we should discuss this at the station, sir, don't you?"

"No, I don't. You have no evidence I was even there," I snap.

"We have a neighbour, says he saw you and gave your name. Apparently, you were fence hopping over the back of the property right as we arrived," he says with a smug grin. Damn neighbours and their twitching blinds.

"Well, it couldn't have been him," says Brook, sidling up to me and tucking herself into my side with a smile. "He was occupied with me." I hold my breath, partly because the cop looks pissed as hell but also because Tanner has his fists balled by his sides. I make a show of my hands, so he knows I'm not touching his ol' lady. "So, I suggest you go and talk to Ginger and then come back when she talks," says Brook, wrapping her arm around my waist and snuggling further into me. The cop scowls and then shakes his head before stomping from the room.

I step away from Brook as soon as they're gone and hold my hands up above my head. "I didn't touch her," I say to Tanner. He ignores me and stares directly at her. She rolls her eyes.

"Don't be ridiculous, I was helping out your brother," she snaps, and he raises his eyebrow in surprise. I don't think I've ever heard Brook use an annoyed tone on Tanner, and by the look on his face, neither has he.

"You wanna say that again," he growls, "with a little less attitude."

"You're being a dick," she snaps, and I suck in a breath, waiting to see Tanner's reaction.

"Seriously, woman, you're pushing your luck," he grits out, taking a step towards her. She moves back, defiance written all over her face.

"You know, Kain would totally have put his arms around me if you weren't such a psychotic nutter," she mutters.

Tanner turns his angry glare to me, and I wave my hands in the air again innocently. "I really wouldn't have, Tan. She's making that up," I rush out, and Brook hits me on the arm.

"You said you'd be all over my arse if Tanner wasn't around," she gasps, and I know by the smirk that she's enjoying pissing Tanner off.

My mouth falls open that she could rat me out like that. "Brother, I was being polite. It was Pres's wedding day and I was just telling her she looked good. Yah know how we speak, it ain't all 'hey, you look nice'. It's more like 'hey, I'd tap that' . . ." I trail off when his eyes blaze with fury. "Seriously, Brook, tame the beast," I growl. "Don't you think I've had enough beatings today?"

"I'll call him off when you tell me the truth," she says with a smug grin. "Did Ginger do that to you today?" I scowl at her underhanded tactics. "Tanner, other men are allowed to look at me. I'm a fine female specimen, and you should be proud you get to take me home. Don't you want other men to look at me and see my beauty?" she asks, twirling around and then poking her backside out. She's totally prodding the bear, and I don't appreciate it.

"Fine," I snap. "Yes, she did." Brook and Tanner both freeze and then look to me to explain. I sigh and shrug. "She isn't well, and she can't help it."

"Yes, she can. If you beat her arse like that, she'd have you up on a charge for battery. You have to tell the cops," says Brook.

"You think those jokers will believe a word I say? A heavy-set, six-foot-tall biker getting beat by a five-foot-something female built like a twig? I'm good with keeping the secret, thanks."

"You have to. What if she blames what happened today on you and you end up back inside?"

"Then I'll be inside and away from all the shit. Suits me just fine."

"Brook, leave it," snaps Tanner when she opens her mouth to protest. She closes it again. "We're here for you, brother, just say the word," he adds, grabbing Brook's wrist. She tries to pull free, but he growls at her. "Jesus, woman, give it up and get upstairs."

"Not a chance. You're not fucking this bad mood out of me," she snaps, and Tanner laughs. He bends slightly and then throws Brook over his shoulder.

"Wanna bet?" he asks, heading for the stairs.

I go to the bar where a few of the brothers are having a drink when Jase turns to me. "Hey, we're gonna check out Marshall's club. You wanna come with?"

I take a beer from behind the bar and reply, "Yeah, why not. Nothing better to do."

Marshall's bar is nice. I haven't been for obvious reasons, but I'm impressed with the place, and I can see why some of the guys come and hang out here. It's still early and the place is quiet as we stand at the bar. "Hey, any service?" shouts Jase. The 'Staff Only' door behind the bar opens and Lacey smiles brightly as she approaches.

"Sorry, boys, I was busy taking care of something. What can I get you?"

"Just give us the bottle of whiskey and six glasses," Jase orders. She nods and goes about getting the order together. We take a seat at the bar, and she watches us carefully. "You want something?" snaps Jase.

"I just wondered whether you all might be more comfortable over there in a booth," she suggests.

"No, we're good here. Now, get lost." She disappears back through the door.

"Harsh, man," says Irish, pouring us each a finger of whiskey.

"She told Kayla about me fucking Kim. I can't stand the bitch," explains Jase. He's just as bad as me when it comes to women. His life is complicated and his ol' lady, Kayla, is crazy. The door swings open again and all the guys turn to me.

"What?" I ask. Jase nods behind the bar, and I follow his direction to find Harper restocking the fridge. I slam my glass on the bar. "What the hell is she doing here?" She's eight months pregnant and working in a strip bar.

Jase shrugs his shoulders. "I didn't know, VP."

I make my way down and lean over the bar. "New job?" I ask, and she jumps in fright, turning to face me.

"Yes," she says. "How are you, Kain?"

"Don't come over all proper like we're just acquaintances, when last week I was balls deep inside you," I growl.

"Really, Kain, I thought we were past all that sniping and bitching." She sighs, looking disappointed.

"We were, but then I find out you lied to me," I snap.

"I didn't lie. I just didn't tell you. Marshall's helping me out, and it's only for another week."

"To hell with that. Get your shit, now. I'm taking you home." Marshall steps out from the back and rolls his eyes when he sees me talking to Harper. "Don't roll your eyes at me," I yell, then look back at Harper. "Why the hell's he eyerolling me?"

"Kain, just stop," she hisses, her face flushing with embarrassment.

"I don't want you working in a fucking strip club," I yell.

"And how am I going to afford a baby as a single parent? You have no say, and you promised you'd back off," she reminds me. "Besides, it isn't like I'm up on stage or anything," she adds, and just that thought alone has me gripping onto the bar to stop myself from dragging her out of here.

"Yah know what, do what you like. You always do anyway," I snap, heading back to my brothers. "Fucking women," I mutter to myself.

CHAPTER TEN

Harper

I pass by the guys. Marshall is sitting with them at the bar, and I catch the back end of his conversation. "No, her parents are cool, although I don't get how they created such perfection. Harper is nothing like either of them." It pisses me off, firstly because I don't want the guys, especially Kain, thinking there's something going on between Marshall and me, and secondly because I know he's doing it purely to piss Kain off, and I'm done with the games.

"Marshall, can I have a word?" I ask coldly. He eyes me warily and then smiles to the rest of the guys before standing and moving to the other side of the bar with me. "Why are you telling the guys about dinner with my parents?"

"It came up," he answers innocently, and I give him my best 'oh really' face. He smiles and then touches my cheek gently. "Because Jase asked me what I did this week, it came up, honestly."

"I don't want you to talk like that in front of Kain. It isn't right."

"Why do you care what he thinks after the way he's treated you?" His tone is angry, and it's not a manner he's ever used with me before.

"Because Kain and I came to an understanding. He's backing off, and now you're trying to piss him off. Just stop. This isn't a game."

"I know it isn't a fucking game," he says. "You think he didn't share details of your recent night together, letting me know how he fucked you all night long?" I gasp. Marshall didn't let on that he knew about that night, and I swore Mila to secrecy, so I know she wouldn't have told anyone. I look over to where Kain sits watching us and my heart hurts.

"I'm done being the prize between you two," I snap. "Leave me out of your petty pissing contest. Both of you, stay away from me," I add, and then I rush to the back room for my break.

I send a text message to Mila and Brook asking for a coffee meet tomorrow morning. I've been practising waking up early so I'm not so cranky when the baby arrives. I've always been a terrible morning person. They both agree to meet me at the coffee shop near my place at nine. I need to focus on myself and the baby, not these childish men.

When I get back out to the bar, the guys have moved over to a booth, Marshall included. A group of girls on a birthday night out have joined them. We often get groups of girls in here. I guess it's the perfect place to pick up men when most of the clientele are male.

"Marshall requested that we serve them at the table," says Milly, and she pulls a face that tells me she can't be bothered with that.

"Requested or ordered?" I ask, and she rolls her eyes. "I'll do it," I offer. "You do enough with dancing and serving," I add, and she kisses me on the cheek.

"Thank you. I really don't want to deal with Jase tonight." I take her notepad and a pen and head over, putting on my best friendly smile, the one I use to get extra tips.

"Good evening, guys and girls, can I get you anything to drink?" I ask brightly. A large pink balloon bops me in the face. I glare at the stupid twenty-one glittering in the lights and wonder if I'll get away with puncturing it with my pen.

"Can we get three bottles of Champagne, please," says Marshall. "And not the cheap shit, Harper. Go down in the cellar and find some of the expensive stuff. We can't have these girls celebrating a twenty-first on cheap champagne." The girls squeal in delight, and Marshall is showered with kisses to the cheek.

"Why are you working here when you're so pregnant?" asks one of the girls. "You look like you could just drop that baby out right here on the floor," she adds, turning to her friend and laughing. Usually, one of the guys would step in for me, but everyone at the table falls silent. I shake my head in disappointment and walk away. I started the evening with two men wanting to look after me, and now, I've managed to piss them both off.

"You good?" asks Milly. I place the notepad on the bar and nod.

"Marshall requested the finest champagne from the cellar." I laugh, and she rolls her eyes. "Could you grab that? It'll take me all night to go up and down those stairs." She laughs and heads for the cellar.

A few minutes later, I place the bucket of ice and Champagne on the table, and Milly sets down a tray of glasses. One of the girls is wrapped around Jase and they're practically eating each other's face off. It pisses me off because I like Jase's ol' lady, Kayla, and I know they've been having difficulties lately, but if she did this, he'd lose his shit. I make a note to mention it to the girls tomorrow to see what they suggest. The ol' ladies usually look out for each other, but seeing as I'm not one, I may get accused of interfering in club business.

"No, I'm completely free and single," Marshall is saying to another of the girls. She's pretty, with the tiniest waist, and I can see why he likes her. Her blonde hair is glossy and curled perfectly, compared to my limp, greasy mess that I've had to pile on top of my head with a hair tie. She looks like a supermodel. Kain is nowhere to be seen, and I wonder if he's gone home to Ginger. The thought depresses me as I take a seat behind the bar to rest.

I wait for them to finish the first bottle of Champagne before I take over the next. The girl is straddling Marshall and whispering into his ear, and he laughs before they both turn to me. I can't hide that it hurts. I don't want Marshall in that way, but he's been a good friend and I'm sad that he can turn cold so easily. It seems to be the way with these Hammers men, rejection doesn't sit well with them.

As I turn to walk away, I run straight into a hard chest. Luckily, I see him just before my stomach hits him. Looking up into Kain's eyes, my heart rate picks up. There's a look on his face that I can't place, but it only takes me a second to figure it out. A brunette moves from behind him and joins the rest of the girls at the booth, and then it hits me—the look on Kain's face is one of guilt and regret.

"Harper, I—" he begins, but I step around him and make my way back to the bar. I shouldn't be upset because Kain isn't mine. He isn't anyone's, apparently.

Brook places the tray of coffees on the table just as Mila arrives. "Sorry I'm late. I had trouble getting out of bed," she says, adding a wink. Brook grins, and I groan. The last thing on my mind right now is sex, yet with these two, it's always a topic we end up discussing.

"What was so urgent that you had to drag us from our beds at this hour?" Brook asks.

"I'm practising living on less sleep," I say. "Ready for when the baby comes."

"I thought you had some exciting gossip that couldn't wait," groans Mila.

I decide to go with talking about Jase first. They clearly need gossip and that's about as juicy as I've got. Mila looks shocked, but Brook doesn't look even vaguely surprised. "Poor Kayla. Should we tell her?" asks Mila.

"No," says Brook while I say, "Yes." We look at each other, and Brook sighs. "She probably already knows, and if we mention it, then it causes problems. Some women accept that their men are just rat bags and they're okay with that." I know what it feels like to keep those kinds of secrets, and I also know that it will kill Mila not to tell Kayla.

"In other news, I told Marshall to leave me alone," I say. "He then spent the rest of the night with his tongue down some girl's throat. It was her twenty-first birthday, so he gave away three bottles of Champagne worth around four hundred notes each, not to mention the cocktails and other drinks they had."

"Ouch. Why'd yah tell him to leave you alone?" asked Mila.

"Because I overheard him telling the guys about our dinner date with my parents. Kain was there, and I thought it was unfair. When I pulled him up on it, he told me that Kain told him about our night together last weekend." Brook's eyes almost bug out of her head and she glares at Mila accusingly. I'd forgotten that she didn't know this snippet of information.

"Did you know about this?" she asks, and Mila winces, a guilty expression on her face.

"I asked her not to tell anyone. I was going to tell you, but I haven't had the chance because Tanner is always glued to your arse," I explain. "So, Marshall was stuck to some girl, and he left with her, and then Kain disappeared for a while and came back from the bathroom with one of the other girls. All in all, it was a great night," I say sarcastically.

"Oh, sweetie," says Mila, placing her hand over mine and rubbing it gently. "Maybe it's a good thing, though, to step away from both of them."

"I'm going to, but it doesn't mean it isn't hurting. Marshall's been a great friend. How can he just turn like that and be so cold?"

"That's a Hammers trait," says Mila. "They can be so cruel when they don't get their own way. Marshall will come around. He's just hurt, especially finding out that you'd slept with Kain."

"Kain is as bad as Jase. He has enough women and yet he's still going after more. Ginger will kill him if she finds out," I say. Brook looks away and stares out the window. "What?" I ask, and she looks at me innocently.

"Nothing."

"You know something," I accuse, and she blushes.

"Kain's got a lot going on right now. The cops turned up at the clubhouse yesterday. A neighbour reported a domestic between him and Ginger. She's been taken to hospital, and I gave Kain an alibi."

I'd noticed more bruises on Kain last night, but he's always covered in them lately, so it's hard to pick out what's new and what's old.

"Is Ginger okay?" I ask. I'm not her biggest fan, but the thought of her being hurt so close to the end of her pregnancy worries me. "Why did you give him an alibi?"

"Because he didn't hurt her," she says firmly, and when I look at her doubtfully, she becomes annoyed. "Harper, you know Kain. You know he wouldn't hurt any woman, especially not one carrying his baby."

"I'm just saying that if she's in hospital and the neighbours called the cops, something must have happened." I don't know why I'm saying this. I do know Kain, and I know deep down that what Brook is saying is true.

"Yes, something did happen, Harper, but Kain didn't hurt Ginger," Brook snaps.

"Then what happened?" asks Mila.

"I can't tell you. It's up to Kain to tell you, but I can promise you that those Hammers boys would never beat on a woman." She loves those men like brothers, and I get why she's defending them.

"Well, it makes no difference to me anymore because I'm out. No more Hammers men, no more bikers, in fact, no more men. It isn't worth it. I just need to focus on me and this baby and forget about finding my Prince Charming because he doesn't exist," I declare. "Would it help if I go and see Ginger and tell her that I'm not trying to steal her man?"

"No," says Brook. "Definitely not. Kain will go mental if you visit Ginger."

"I think it's a good idea," says Mila. "It can't hurt, and maybe it'll be one less obstacle that she has to stress about. I know she doesn't know about the baby being Kain's, but we all think she suspects, so maybe hearing that you're out of the picture will reassure her. You could be the reason they're arguing." I nod in agreement with Mila. It can only help, and I guess a small part of me needs to release some of this guilt that I'm carrying around for ruining their relationship.

CHAPTER ELEVEN

Kain

I sweep up the mess in the bedroom. I've contacted the hospital, and they're keeping Ginger in for observation. They have her medical records and know her history. It's obvious she is struggling, and they mentioned that her blood pressure was far too high for a woman in her condition. I'm hoping they keep her until she's had the baby so she can get the right care, because I'm running out of options.

My mobile beeps, indicating I have a text message, and I see it's a message from my cousin thanking me for last night. She'd rang me because the bar they'd booked for her friend's twenty-first birthday had closed an hour before they were due there, so I'd invited her to Legz with Marshall's permission, and we made sure they had a good night.

I head into the club, hoping that Cooper has a run for me or at least a debt collection. I need to work off some of this stress. When I arrive, Cooper and Mila are in the middle of a full-blown argument. She's screaming at him about keeping secrets, and he's shouting back about it being club business and that he doesn't tell any ol' ladies about club business. I wince at how he words it, knowing this will only piss her off more. When Mila sets her eyes on me, I begin to back out of the main room because she's clearly in a bad mood and is looking for a new target.

"You," she hisses, moving after me. "Don't you think you have enough on with Ginger and Harper without adding more women to the list?" I instantly know she's talking about last night and the fact that Harper saw me come back inside the bar with my cousin. Harper didn't let me explain then, and I'm pretty sure Mila won't let me explain now, so I roll my eyes with a bored expression and go into the bar.

Joe and Sam look at me with sympathy as Joe hands me a whiskey. "She's been screaming like that for the last half-hour," he says, shaking his head.

"Yeah?" I sigh. "It's not like Cooper to stand for it. He must be going soft."

"How's Ginger?" asks Sam.

I shrug. "I haven't been to see her. I'll only make her worse, and she doesn't need the stress. They're keeping her in for obs."

"And how's Harper?" asks Joe. "We miss her around here." I feel guilty because the brothers really did love having Harper around. She kept them in order.

"She's working over at Legz," I say. "Against my advice," I add.

"I think it was nice of her to go and see Ginger, though. Shows that she's moving on and making things right," says Joe, and Sam nods in agreement.

I glance between them. "What are you talking about?"

"Erm, Mila said something to Cooper just now about Harper needing closure, and if she wanted to see Ginger, that was her choice. Cooper ain't happy, of course, and said you'd be pissed, but you look calm to me," says Joe.

"That's because this is the first time I've heard about it," I growl, storming back into the clubhouse. Cooper has Mila pressed against the far wall and he's talking into her ear. She suddenly looks less angry and more turned-on. "I hate to ruin the moment, but what the fuck is Harper thinking going to see Ginger?" They both turn to me, and Cooper closes his eyes in annoyance.

"It's nothing to do with you," snaps Mila.

"Fuck you, Mila, it's everything to do with me. Ginger isn't well and she doesn't need that kind of stress," I growl.

"Get in the office," Cooper orders, pulling Mila by the arm. I follow, and he slams the door closed. "We don't need this spilling out into the club. I've made her text Harper and call it off, but it's too late, brother. She's already at the hospital."

"She only wants to tell her that she's backing off, that she's not standing in her way anymore. She felt bad when she heard you'd had a huge argument, and she's worried that Ginger will press charges to spite you," explains Mila. I don't stay around to listen to anymore, instead running from the clubhouse and jumping on my bike. I need to stop this clusterfuck before it gets out of hand.

Harper

I report to the nurse on the desk. She looks tired, but she smiles up at me anyway. "I'm here to see Virginia Shaw," I say.

She frowns. "I'm sorry, but she isn't taking visitors right now. Can I ask who you are?" My phone beeps with a text. I glance at it and see Mila is asking if I'm at the hospital yet. I shoot a text back telling her I am and then I turn it off and stuff it back in my pocket.

"It's really important that I speak to her. Can you ask if she wants to speak to me? I'm Harper." The nurse contemplates my request, and then, with a nod, she stands and disappears into a room opposite her desk. A minute later, she pops her head out the door and smiles. I go into the room and find Ginger sitting up in the hospital bed. She looks pale and tired. The dark circles under her eyes tell me she isn't sleeping, and as I take a seat by the bed, her hollow eyes fall to me.

"Hey," I say with a smile. "How're you feeling?"

"That's not why you're here," she mutters. "What do you want?"

"Erm, I just . . ." I trail off because, suddenly, my mouth feels dry and my words have evaded me.

"Can you give this to Kain?" she asks, reaching to her side table and passing me a white envelope. I take it and pop it into my bag, nodding. "He hasn't been to see me," she says, her eyes falling to the window. Her tone seems to have changed, now almost wistful. "I knew it was true. He didn't ever really love me."

"Ginger, he—" I begin, but she laughs manically, cutting me off.

"He loves Harper. Her and her perfect fucking baby," she spits out, and I'm confused. It's like she doesn't know who I am.

"Actually, I came to tell you that he does love you. He wants to be with you and your baby," I say, and her eyes drop back to me. "Harper isn't going to stand in the way anymore," I add.

"It doesn't matter. He won't forgive me, not now."

"Why? What did you do?" I ask.

"I lied and told the nice cop that Kain beats me." She sighs, and I gasp. "He took a statement from me today. Kain's on borrowed time." She laughs again and rubs a hand over her swollen bump. "All the times he let me beat him, he's not man enough to hurt me." Her tone is bitter and my heart aches for Kain. I need to get to him and tell him, but when I stand, she glares at me. "What are you doing in here?" she growls. "Why are you in my room?"

"Sorry, I'm leaving," I say, heading for the door. She's clearly sicker than Kain let on. As my hand pushes on the door, she shouts out, halting me.

"Is it true? Is your baby Kain's? Lacey told me that it's Kain's." I look back at her and nod once. She lets out a scream and begins pinching at her stomach. The door slams open, and the nurse comes in closely followed by Kain.

He glares at me and roars, "What the hell did you say?"

"Nothing. I . . . she . . ." I watch as he tries to help the nurse get control of her arms. She hits herself in the stomach, screaming and yelling. The nurse presses an alarm button, and I slowly back from the room, my eyes fixed on the chaos. I'm shoved to the side and the room is suddenly filled with cops all shouting to Kain to get on his knees. Kain's eyes meet mine as he falls to his knees and places his hands on top of his head as instructed. He's cuffed and one of the cops reads his rights while they pull him roughly to his feet.

"Do you see?" he snarls at me. "Do you see what you've done?"

"I didn't. I just—"

"Get out of my fucking sight. I don't want to ever see you again." The venom in his voice is cutting, and I instinctively rub a hand over my heart where I feel it break in two. "You're dead to me, you and that fucking kid," he spits out as they drag him from the room. I stagger to the nearby seats and lower myself into one.

I watch as they pull him down the hallway and he struggles against his restraints. He suddenly lunges forward, headbutting one of the cops, and all hell breaks loose again as they take him to the floor and each grab a limb. I turn away, not wanting to see the fight he's causing because he's angry.

I stay sitting in the hallway for some time. Kain is long gone after they carried him out of the hospital in restraints. I called it through to Cooper, and no doubt the club will get Kain a good solicitor and he'll be back out in no time. The nurse informed me that Ginger was sedated. I was worried for the baby, but she assured me that it was the only way to keep her from hurting herself and the baby.

The nurse approaches and hands me a cup of tea. She sits next to me, and I smile at her gratefully. "Heavy day," she says with a sigh, and I laugh. That's an understatement. "Is there anyone I can call to come and collect you?" she offers.

"No, I drove here. I'll get out of your way," I say.

"You're not doing any harm here, and I don't mind if you want more time to sit. We'll look after her though," she reassures me, nodding towards Ginger's room.

"Is she crazy?" I ask. It's been playing on my mind because Ginger wasn't herself. What Brook said about Kain not hurting Ginger was true. It's been the other way around all along.

"Crazy isn't really a word we use these days," she says, "and I can't discuss her medical condition with you, unless she's your family."

"I'm her sister," I try, and she laughs.

"Nice try. Look, she'll be okay. Her condition is treatable, but while she's pregnant, it's harder to control. The doctors are discussing a C-section. Once the baby is out, we can medicate her." I realise that if I want answers, I'll need to go to Cooper. I smile and stand, thanking her for everything, and then I leave.

It's getting dark outside. I must have sat there for a few hours. I text Mila and ask if there's any sign of Kain at the clubhouse as I want to pop by. She texts back that he's still locked up.

When I arrive, Mila is waiting in the bar for me. She jumps off her stool and comes towards me. "What happened?"

"I shouldn't have gone there. Ginger isn't well at all."

"Okay, in what way?" She leads me to a table, and we sit down. I relay to her how Ginger behaved and how erratic she was. "Brook was right. It wasn't him smashing things up and being violent. It was her, she told me."

"But he's been arrested," says Mila. Cooper approaches, looking stressed and pissed-off. "Baby, Harper said Ginger admitted to her that she was lying to the cops."

Cooper takes a seat. "It makes no difference. The cops wouldn't believe you. I've contacted the solicitor, and she says she can get the whole thing kicked out of court since Ginger isn't well enough to make a statement. My man on the inside says Kain isn't in a good way. He's in solitary right now because he won't calm down. They won't let him out until he calms."

"He was really mad at me," I say. "I was only trying to help him, Cooper."

"I don't know why you thought it would be a good idea to go and see her. You slept with her ol' man behind her back and got pregnant. What did you think would happen? Was you expecting a cup of tea and to make friends?" I glance at Mila, and she turns to Cooper.

"I told Harper it was a good idea. We thought Ginger would want to know that Harper is done with Kain. She was just trying to make things right."

Cooper puts his head in his hands and groans. "Christ, Mila. I tell you not to get involved and the first thing you do is get involved. Why can't you do as you're told for once in your damn life?" Mila looks pissed and her eyes widen. "You aren't just an ol' lady around here, you're married to the President. You can't get involved in the little dramas."

"Carry on talking to me like a child and we won't be married for much longer," she hisses.

"Guys, don't argue." I sigh, so over them arguing. "I'm gonna get out of here before Kain gets out. He doesn't want to see me, and I can imagine it will be a while before he's calm enough to talk. If you need anything from me, just call," I say, rising to my feet. Cooper gives a nod. "And if you talk to him, tell him I'm sorry. I thought I was helping."

CHAPTER TWELVE

Kain

I sign the paperwork and push it back across the desk to the officer. He looks it over before handing over my belongings in a plastic Ziplock, then I step outside into the fresh air. Cooper is waiting in his truck, and I smile gratefully. "How's it going, brother?" He grins, and we shake hands. I pass over the regards sent by various prisoners to Cooper, and we chat about what's happening inside. It's been a while since any of the brothers have been there, and so we've lost touch with that world.

"Any news on Ginger?" I ask. Cooper sighs and shakes his head.

"No, and you can't go there. One of your bail conditions is that you stay away from her. I've got the solicitor on it, and she thinks we can quash the whole thing and clear your name, but don't break the conditions." Joanne is the club's lawyer. She's damn good at what she does, and although she costs a fortune, she's worth every penny. "Harper came by the club," adds Cooper, glancing across at me.

"I don't wanna talk about Harper," I snap.

"What happened?"

"What do you think happened? She told Ginger about her and the baby. I never thought she could be so cruel and heartless. I told her Ginger wasn't well, and she did that knowing that Ginger was at her lowest."

"To be honest, brother, I don't think she was trying to cause trouble. I think she wanted to help. She was trying to tell Ginger that she wasn't involved with you anymore, that she was stepping away." That just makes it worse in my eyes, and if she was so desperate to sort things, she should have spoken to me first. All I see is that Harper wanted to clear her own conscience. She didn't think about me or Ginger in that, or the implications her actions would have.

"No offence, Coop, but I don't want to talk about it. She knew what she was doing, and I saw a different side to her, one I've no interest in knowing. Harper and I are done."

"And the baby?" he asks, and I shrug. I told Harper I wasn't interested, but I've spent the last three days thinking about the whole situation. My kid shouldn't miss out on having a father because of its mother. Maybe in time we can come to an arrangement, but right now, I have no desire to see Harper.

We get back to the clubhouse, and I'm met with cheers from the brothers. A whiskey is thrust into my hand, and someone turns up the jukebox. I can't see Ginger, so I may as well relax tonight and celebrate my freedom, just in case the solicitor doesn't clear my name and I end up back behind bars, paying for a crime I haven't committed.

Later, some of the brothers want to go to Legz. The thought of seeing Harper pisses me off, but there's a tiny flicker deep inside that needs to see her. It's almost like an addiction, and I don't know if my need to see her is so I can lay into her or if I just need to work out my feelings, and so I agree. She may not even be on shift tonight.

Legz is busy. We queue at the bar for over ten minutes, and I stay to the back so I don't have to face Harper if she's there. Max passes me a whiskey and then we head to a booth. Woody brings over a girl who's blonde and attractive. "To celebrate your freedom, brother." He laughs, holding her hand above her head and twirling her around in front of me. I catch a glimpse of Harper watching me from behind the bar, and so I take the girl's hand and pull her towards me. I lay my wallet on the table and nod for her to go ahead and dance. I'm not interested in seeing this woman's body, but I want to hurt Harper in the way she's hurt me.

The night continues in the same manner. I drink shot after shot and then wash that down with whiskey. Girls continue to come to our booth and dance for us. I lose track of the amount of money we lay out for that shit, but it must be good because they keep on coming. Harper keeps her distance, remaining behind the bar. It's the first time we've ever been in the same room and haven't interacted at all, not even to snipe at each other. An outsider wouldn't know we were acquaintances let alone ex-lovers.

Towards the end of the evening, Harper approaches to clear our table. She makes polite conversation with the guys, and when she goes to leave, I grab her by the arm. It's a hard grip and I know I must be hurting her, but my drunken brain has put my arse head firmly on. "I thought I told you to stay away from me," I slur.

"Hey, come on, Kain, don't be a dick," says Jase. I ignore him and stare up at Harper.

"You came to my workplace. I can't avoid you if you're here when I have to work."

"But you don't have to work, do you? I've seen what's in your bank account, almost forty-five thousand pounds." Harper looks shocked, but it's standard practise for Cooper to run checks on his employees, so we knew when she came to the MC for the bar job that she was loaded. "So, tell me why you insist on working almost up until you're about ready to give birth?"

Harper fidgets uncomfortably and tries to pull her wrist free, but I squeeze harder and she winces. "Kain, let go, you're hurting me."

"Well, you thought I was a wife beater anyway, so I may as well live up to expectations. Isn't that what you told Brook, that the cops wouldn't come for me unless there was a good reason?" Brook was upset by Harper's lack of faith in me, and I overheard her spilling to Tanner about their argument.

"I know you're upset and I'll talk about this with you, but not right now, not when your arse is drunk and you're looking at me like you want to hurt me," she hisses. "Now, get the fuck off my wrist or I swear to God I will scream this place down. I guarantee even the VP of the Hammers won't get special treatment from our security here." I can't help the smile that creeps over my face. It's been a while since I've seen such fire in her eyes. I release her wrist and watch her stomp away.

"Man, that was a shit move," says Max, and I glare at him. He has no idea what she's done, what trouble she's caused.

ell

The following morning, I wake at home. Usually, I'd sleep at the club and so I have no idea why I'm here or how I got here. I lift myself up slowly, my head spinning, and glance around the room. There's a buzzing noise, but I can't locate it, so I groan and bury my head back into my pillow.

Sometime later, there's a bang and I sit up quickly to find Cooper standing in the room staring down at me. "Get up. Do you not hear your damn phone?" he growls. I place a hand over my mouth, unsure if I'm going to vomit as my hangover is in full force.

"What are you doing here?" I mumble.

"I've been calling you for over an hour. I got a call from the hospital, Ginger's hurt herself. We have to get there." I dive out of bed and pull on my denim jeans. I stuff my feet in my boots and grab my shirt, pulling it on as I follow Cooper from the room, all thoughts of my hangover forgotten.

We arrive at the hospital after Cooper managed to get the solicitor to get special permission so I could break the no contact order. The hospital has me as next of kin on Ginger's record, and because of the baby, a judge lifted the order temporarily. We're taken into a side room and asked to wait for the doctor.

"Did they say what she'd done?" I ask, and Cooper shakes his head. Mila comes in and smiles at me sympathetically. Cooper tucks her into his side as I pace the room. "I hope the baby's okay," I mutter. I know she tried several times to punch her stomach, but she never said the words out loud, so I was never really certain if it was just anger and frustration or if she actually wanted to hurt the baby. The door finally opens, and a doctor comes in. His face is sad and he looks tired.

"Mr. Morgan, I'm Doctor Harris. I've been taking care of Virginia Shaw." We shake hands. He suddenly looks nervous, and it makes me anxious. "I'm afraid I have some bad news. Ms. Shaw passed away shortly after noon today." I stare at the doctor. The words hit my brain, and I continue to stare. What does he mean passed away? Ginger passed away? I frown, my face full of confusion, and I look over to Cooper. He looks just as confused, and Mila begins to cry. "I know this must come as a huge shock, it took us all by surprise, but a nurse found her with open wounds to her arms at eleven-thirty this morning. Her pulse was very weak, and we worked hard to get her back, but unfortunately, she fought us hard and her heart stopped beating twice. By the third attempt to revive her, she was completely gone."

"I don't under . . . I thought she was safe here. What open wounds?" I manage to ask.

"She was under two hourly observations. The nurse last checked her at ten o'clock. She reported that Ms. Shaw was alert and much happier today. Her mood was improved, and she seemed relaxed. The nurse was free at eleven-thirty, and so she popped in to see if Ms. Shaw needed anything and she found her unresponsive."

"What did she do?" asks Cooper.

"She cut her wrists significantly. Her wounds ran from her hand to her elbow on her inner arm. She then wrapped them loosely in sheets, which we believe she did to hide any blood that may have alerted us but not to stop the bleeding."

"She meant to do it. It wasn't a cry for help. She wanted to die," mutters Mila, her sobs slipping out between words.

The doctor nods in agreement. "Of course, that's only speculation, looking back at her records and her recent behaviour. The coroner would have to compile a full report and conclude what happened."

"So, you're telling me that Ginger is dead . . . she's died?" I ask, suddenly feeling a rage fill my heart. "You were supposed to look after her, keep her safe. How the fuck did she get something sharp enough to cut herself? I told you she was self-harming, why the hell was she left around sharps?" I yell, stepping close to the doctor. Cooper jumps in between us, pushing me back against the wall and holding me there.

"Calm down, brother. This man tried to save her," he warns, growling the words close to my ear.

"What about the baby?" asks Mila, and I freeze. In all the confusion, I hadn't even thought about the baby. I wait for the words, to hear that my baby is dead, but he takes a deep breath and smiles a little.

"Your baby is just fine. He was born healthy and alert last night. Ms. Shaw said that she'd informed you," he says. "I can take you to him now."

Cooper slaps me on the back. "You're a daddy, brother. Congratulations."

It feels bittersweet. I have a son, but I've lost his mother. What will I tell him when he's old enough to ask for her?

I'm taken into a nursery full of plastic cots and screaming babies. A nurse leads me over to the farthest crib, where a tiny baby is sleeping soundly. He isn't crying or fussing. He's wrapped up cosy in a blue blanket with 'Baby Shaw' scrawled in chalk above the cot. The nurse reaches in and picks him up.

He doesn't stir as she hands him to me. "He's quite something," she says with a smile. "All this noise and he just sleeps. He wakes, he lays quietly until I feed him, and then he sleeps some more." I manage a small smile, and she leaves me alone with the sleeping bundle.

I find a rocking chair in the corner of the room. Settling into it, I look down at his tiny face. He's perfect, and I know every parent thinks that about their own kid, but he really is perfect. His little rosebud mouth moves like he's mimicking feeding time, and I become transfixed on each little twitch.

Eventually, the nurse comes over holding out a bottle. "It's feeding time," she says and smiles. I've never fed a baby. I've never even held a baby this small until now. When she sees the horror on my face, she laughs and pulls up a stool. "It's easy, I'll help you," she offers.

CHAPTER THIRTEEN

Harper

I cry real, heart-wrenching sobs that shake my entire body. My heart aches for the baby that will now have to grow up without his mum, and every time I picture that, I cry some more. Mila rubs gentle circles on my back. "It's just so sad," I sob, and she nods in agreement. "Is Kain okay?"

"He's getting on with it, but he doesn't have a choice. The baby is allowed home tomorrow and then he's flying solo. Of course, he'll have the support of his brothers, and he's going to stay at the clubhouse so that the ol' ladies can help out. The baby will be so well looked after. Everyone is heartbroken," says Mila.

"Should I go and see him?" I ask.

"Sweetie, he's got enough on. He'll call if he needs you," she says softly, and I know she's just trying to let me down gently. He doesn't want to see me, and I don't blame him.

I slide down to the floor of the bedroom that the guys decorated for the baby. It's cream in colour. I didn't find out the baby's sex, so it'll be a surprise. I stroke my pencil against the cream wall and draw out the bunny from *Peter Rabbit*. It's been a long time since I drew anything, but I have to take my mind off Kain and Ginger. The time passes quickly, and before I know it, I've drawn a whole scene of bunnies in the farmer's field stealing the vegetables.

By lunchtime, I've drawn myself into a stupor and I drop my pencil on the floor. The clatter it makes rings out around the emptiness of the house. I pull myself up into the rocking chair and sob. For Ginger, for Kain, and for their baby.

I sit for some time, ugly crying to myself, and I'm surprised when the bedroom door opens and Mila enters. She rushes to my side, dropping to her knees and wrapping me in a hug.

"My heart hurts for them, Mila," I sob. She rubs my back gently, crying with me.

"I know, sweetie. It's awful," she whispers.

"How is he?"

"He's pretty closed off, to be honest. He sits all day with the baby in the nursery. It's been two days now since Ginger passed and he's only left the hospital to wash and change. He'll only leave the baby if a certain nurse is there. I guess his possessive side is taking over and carrying him through."

"I want to see him. Do you think he'll want to see me?" I ask. I know by her expression that she doesn't think it's a good idea. "But he needs someone," I sob.

"I don't think that person is you right now, sweetie." She sighs sympathetically. "He's shutting everyone out and he specifically told you to stay away." I nod in agreement. Kain would probably take his mood out on me right now. "Wow, I love this," she says, pushing to her feet and stroking her fingers over the new artwork. "You'll be a great mum, Harp," she adds with a soft smile.

I unlock the door to Gloria and my father's house. She texted me to say she's got some things for the baby. "Hello?" I shout out.

"Finally," says Anton, stepping into view.

"Your mum texted me. Is she around?" I ask.

"Nope, she popped out. She said you might stop by. Luckily for me, I need to talk with you." He points to the kitchen, so I head that way, confused as to why he would want to talk to me. "I met your mum," he says, and I freeze.

"Sorry?" I ask. My father told Gloria that my mum was in a hospital ill, mentally.

"Yeah, she looked well considering she's supposed to be strung out on meds and in a secure hospital. Their house is amazing. I love the glass windows that surround the place. It's like a crystal castle." I eye him warily. He looks calm yet I know that glint in his eye can be dangerous. "And, boy, can she fuck," he adds. I suck in a breath, horror on my face.

"What?" I ask, my voice almost a whisper. He opens his mobile and holds it out to me. Sure enough, there's a video of my mother writhing around on top of a male. The camera turns to show a smug-looking Anton. Tears fill my eyes. My whole life is such a mess, and this is the final straw.

"She picked me up in a bar," he says. "I'll admit, I was giving her the eye cos a cougar like her deserves at least one night of fun."

"Why are you telling me all of this?" I snap.

"Because you knew, and you kept the secrets and the lies. You sat opposite my mother, my beautiful, kind mother, and you lied to her. You're as bad as him," he grits out, poking a finger in my face.

"What was I supposed to do? I was just a kid when I found out, and he threatened me. I was terrified of him."

"Yeah, yeah." He sighs in a bored tone. "The presents helped ease that, though," he adds.

"I was just a kid. I didn't realise what those presents meant back then. I didn't understand bribery. He lied, he did all of this, so go and see him. Show him that video."

"I should," he nods, "I should tear your family apart like you did mine."

"I didn't, he did," I yell.

"And you helped. My mother felt sorry for him. She thought she was taking in a heartbroken guy, sad over his crazy, mentally ill wife. She wanted to help look after you and care for you." I nod as tears pour down my face once again. He's right. I remember my father introducing me to Gloria and she was lovely, down to earth, exactly how I pictured a mum to be. "And all the time, you were both liars!"

"I'm sorry. I don't know how to make this right." I sob, and he glares at me with pure hatred in his eyes.

"You can't. I'm going to ruin you and him, piece by piece. I just wanted you to know that I'm coming."

"What does that even mean? I'll just go and talk to Gloria. I'll tell her everything." Even though the thought of breaking Gloria's heart hurts me.

Anton laughs, moving closer and twisting a lock of my hair around his finger. "If you do, I'll slit your mother's throat." I stare after him as he leaves, gobsmacked. How did I even get here? This is my father's fault and yet again my mother is the one being threatened. My mum and Gloria are innocent in all of this.

I head straight for my father's office. He needs to sort this out, and Anton never said I couldn't tell my father about it. I storm past his secretary despite her objections. I stomp through his unlocked office door to find my father sat back on his leather office chair, his head tilted back in pleasure and a girl younger than me on her knees before him. He sits up quickly, almost knocking the young girl on her naked arse. His surprised face soon turns to anger when he sees me. "What the hell?" he yells. His secretary runs in after me, repeating apologies to him.

"She wouldn't listen. She just came straight past me," she says. He stands, tucking himself away, and then throws some clothes at the young girl.

"Out," he says to me, shoving me from the office and back towards one of the conference rooms. "What the hell do you think you're playing at?"

"Anton knows about Mum," I say, spinning angrily to face him. "He just threatened her, that if I tell Gloria everything, he'll slit Mum's throat."

My father looks stressed and rubs at his brow in confusion. "Start again," he snaps.

"Anton went to see Mum. He's been in the house, and he knows she's well and not in a mental hospital," I grit out.

"So, what? It means nothing. I could say she was better and living her life. There's no proof I'm still with her."

"Oh my god, just stop. Stop with the lies. You've been found out, and now, he's threatening to bring our worlds down. He blames me just as much as you."

"I'll speak to him and even it all out. Don't worry. He isn't capable of slitting anyone's throat or bringing our lives down. You're overreacting. He's always been an angry little fucker."

"Because he knew you were a liar. He's been waiting years to catch you out and now he has. He hates me, and I don't blame him. I'm going to tell Gloria. It's the only way to make this all stop." I turn to leave, but he grabs my upper arm, digging his fingers into the skin and hurting me.

"You won't tell anyone. I'll deal with Anton. If Gloria finds out from you, I'll make your mother pay." It's the threat he's always used, but right now, I'm sick of being the one holding all the secrets. I can't help thinking how similar my situation is with Kain and Ginger. I was the secret and look how that ended.

I push at my father and free myself, then I feel the most crushing pain in my stomach. It makes me fall forward and grip onto the table.

A wetness leaks from between my legs, and I look down in horror as water pools at my feet.

"Oh, Christ, I think I'm in labour," I mutter. My father rushes to my side, pulling out his mobile phone.

"Who do I call?" he asks. I straighten myself and think about that question. I don't have Marshall or Kain, and I'd never really thought about who I'd call.

"Call Mila," I say. I can always count on her.

Kain

I strap the tiny bundle into the car seat. Ginger had purchased most of the baby stuff months ago, and I'm thankful for that because I wouldn't have had a clue. It's time to take the baby home and I'm scared as hell. I've never looked after a baby before. Not only that, I have the court date from the charges hanging over me and I can't help but worry that I'll get locked up and then what will happen to him.

Katie, the nurse I've befriended, leans into the car seat and place a kiss on the baby's head. She smiles up at me. "You're going to be great. Here's my number in case you need anything." She winks at me, and I smile. If I wasn't such a mess right now, I'd totally give her my number so we could hook up.

Cooper's convinced me to go back to the clubhouse for now. Mila will be there to help me out, along with the other ol' ladies. It's a nice gesture, but half of me wants to take the baby to the house I shared with Ginger and lock ourselves away. I want to take care of him and keep the rest of the world away. I requested that under no circumstances were they to celebrate our arrival. The last thing I want is a party, and luckily, when I arrive, the place is quiet with just the ol' ladies waiting to coo over the new addition. I keep a hold on the car seat, not ready to hand him over yet, and the ladies seem to understand because they back off quickly. Eventually, Mila squeezes my arm, "It's okay, Kain, I'll take good care of him. You go and talk with Cooper." I nod and release the car seat to Mila. I know I can trust them all, that they'll help me, but I just don't feel ready to share him.

Cooper shuts the office door, and we sit. "So," he says, leaving the silence hanging.

"I need to arrange the funeral," I say.

"Already done, brother," says Cooper, and I smile, relieved that I have him to look out for me. I was dreading the funeral arrangements. "She's having a good send-off, Kain. I've made sure she has the best of everything." I nod. Ginger didn't have any family, not that she spoke of anyway, so it will be mainly the Hammers family that attend. "It's on Friday. I know that's only two days' notice, but I didn't want to bother you with the details at the hospital. You had enough on. Have you got a name yet?" I shake my head.

It's something we never discussed, and I hate myself for that. Normal couples talk about that shit, but I have no idea what Ginger wanted to call her own baby. "There's no rush. You'll come up with something."

The door opens and Mila comes in holding the baby. "I have to go. Something's come up." She hands the bundle to me, and I hold him to my chest. Cooper stands and rounds the desk to Mila.

"What's come up?"

"I'll tell you later," she says, going to leave, but he grabs hold of her and tugs her back to him.

"Mila," he warns, and she glances between me and Cooper.

"It's Harper," she says, and my ears prick up even though I don't move an inch, "She's gone into labour." She watches me for a reaction, but I don't give her one. Harper is the reason Ginger is dead, the reason my child doesn't have a mother. I shut down any feelings I had for her the day I was arrested.

"Right, well, go. Call me with any news," says Cooper, kissing her on the head. "You not gonna be there?" asks Cooper once Mila is gone.

"Why would I?" I ask coldly.

Cooper eyes me warily, choosing his words. "Because despite what you feel about Harper right now, this is still your baby and it's a sibling to that little bundle of joy you have right there."

"I have one kid—this one." I stand, clutching the baby to me. "I have to feed him."

I'm sitting in the main room much later, the baby asleep on my chest as I watch some show about World War Two with Tanner at my side when Mila returns. She looks tired and stressed. Brook jumps up and rushes over to her. "I was getting worried when I didn't hear anything."

Mila's eyes fill with tears as she shakes her head like her words are stuck in her throat. I resist the urge I have to go over because it's not my business. Brook takes Mila away to the office. "Shit, man, you think Harper is alright?" asks Tanner, and I shrug. "How do you do that, man?" he questions. "Just switch off your feelings for her like that?"

"Easy. I picture the way Ginger screamed as she hit herself over and over because of what Harper told her," I say coldly. Tanner raises his eyebrows and presses his lips together. I sound harsh, but I don't care. I might have to force myself to stay in this seat and not beg Mila to tell me what's happened, but that feeling will pass with time.

Once the baby is settled into his crib, I pull Silk from the room. She giggles as I push her into the bathroom. She's a new club girl, and I've yet to experience her pussy. She's naked within a second of me getting her in the bathroom. I spin her away from me, because I don't want to kiss her, I just need to bury myself into some willing pussy and forget about everything for a while.

She gasps as I ease myself into her, the condom in place, because there's no way I'm getting trapped in the same situation again. I don't wait for her to adjust before I begin moving, taking what I need, not caring if she gets what she needs. I haven't had sex since I took Harper up to Sam's cabin, but I don't feel embarrassed when I'm climaxing within minutes into Silk. The guys were right—her pussy feels just like silk, hence her nickname. She smiles back at me over her shoulder. I pull out and dispose of the condom and then I slap her arse. "Out," I snap. She looks disappointed, but she's been used exactly how she's supposed to be. It's what club arse is for, and there's no point in her getting disillusioned by me being nice.

CHAPTER FOURTEEN

Harper

My whole body aches. No one warned me that labour would take it out on me so bad. I'm tired and sore. The doctors performed a C-section after ten hours of labour. My body was tired, and the baby wasn't really going anywhere. Each push made no difference, and then the heart rate began to drop, so they decided on an emergency section. It was a relief, if I'm honest. But all those days spent thinking about how I was going to push my baby into the world and lay breastfeeding gracefully straight after soon went out the window.

Her small cries fill the room again, and I sigh. She literally cries all the time. I gingerly reach out to the plastic cot and wince as my stitches pull. Hooking my finger onto the plastic, I pull it gently so that it wheels closer to me. A nurse enters just in time, and I relax back into the pillow with relief. "She certainly likes to cry," she comments, and I nod.

"It's been every five minutes." I sigh as the nurse picks her up and hands her to me. I pull up my top and place her to my breast, grimacing as she latches on to my already sore nipple. "Yah know, I might try giving her a bottle next time. I'm really sore," I say.

"It's your decision. I know I'm supposed to push the breastfeeding, but I know what it's like, and I say, do it if you can, but if you struggle, then I'm happy to get you a bottle."

"You have kids?" I ask, and she nods.

"Yeah, just the one. He's a handful. I'm a single mum, so working shifts and trying to take care of Jack is hard, but I love it."

"I'm a single mum too," I admit, suddenly feeling like this is a secret club. "I'm scared to death," I say.

"It's quite common," laughs the nurse kindly, "but you'll get through it. You have an amazing friend," she says, referring to Mila, who's been to visit every day so far. "Yah know, we just released a baby with his father after the mum died. Now, that's gotta be hard."

My mind goes to Kain, and I realise that maybe she's talking about him. I nod in agreement. "To be honest, he was kind of hot, and it's so unprofessional of me, but I gave him my number. Sometimes you can't pass up an opportunity like that," she says with a wink.

"Yeah," I say. "Did he call?"

"Not yet, but I'm praying every day that he does." She leaves the room, and I flop my head back into the pillow. Even the nurses want Kain.

Later, Mila snuggles with the baby as I rummage through my handbag for a tissue. "The nurse looking after me totally hit on Kain," I say.

"Wow, even knowing that Ginger had just died?" asks Mila, screwing up her face with distain.

"She's a single mum, he's a single dad, I guess she saw it as an opportunity," I say. My hand falls onto an envelope and I pull it out and gasp. It's the envelope that Ginger asked me to pass to Kain. I'd forgotten about it. "Oh, I forgot I had this. It's for Kain," I say, holding it to Mila. "Ginger asked me to give it to him when I went to see her," I add. Kain will be even more pissed at me thinking I withheld that on purpose. Mila puts it into her own bag, promising to pass it to him as soon as she arrives home.

"The funeral is tomorrow," she says, "and then Kain's up before the judge on Monday."

"Does the solicitor still think she can get the charges quashed even though Ginger is dead?" I ask.

"She's not as hopeful. It's his word against a ghost. Ginger's statement to the cops was pretty cruel."

"What will happen to the baby if he goes back inside?"

"Well, the solicitor said the least he can hope for is a three-year sentence, and it's up to the courts what happens to the baby seeing as neither of them have family to pass him to. Cooper said we'll take him, of course, but I don't have long left until this one arrives." She sighs, rubbing her bump. "I don't know how we'll cope with Asher, our baby, and then Kain's baby. I think the club will have to pull together."

"I'll help wherever I can. Did you tell Kain about the baby?" I ask.

She shakes her head. "In all honesty, I haven't really seen much of him. He locks himself away most of the time. He wants to do everything for the baby himself. I hear he's screwing around with the club girls again, back to his old ways I guess." She shrugs. It hurts my heart, but I shake the feeling away. We aren't together, so he can do what he likes.

Once Mila has gone, I pull out my mobile phone. I want him to know about Willow. She deserves to be on his radar, and if he's capable of taking care of his son while fucking club girls, then he should know he also has a daughter. I take a close-up picture of her tiny little face and send it to him. Why should he get to ignore her when she's innocent in all of this? I wait to check that he's received it, and when the tick appears next to the picture, I close the screen, turning the mobile off. I know he won't reply, but at least he's seen her now.

The following morning, the doctor signs my release papers. I'm happy to be going home, even though the thought of being alone with Willow is scary. Mila has promised to be around for me, but I know I can't totally rely on everyone else. I chose to have my baby knowing it would be as a single parent and I'm determined to do that.

When I arrive home, the place feels musty and damp. I go around opening all the windows to air the place. I've only been away a few days, but it feels like I'd abandoned it for months.

I lay Willow in the basket that I set up in the living room. Thankfully, she settles nicely, and I take the time to rest up. My mind wanders to Kain and the funeral taking place later today. I feel like I should go and pay my respects, but I'm not sure how Kain would react to me being there.

There's a knock on the door and I groan. It takes me some time to ease off the couch, but when I finally get to the door, I find Marshall, which surprises me. The last time we saw each other, he was a complete dick. He shifts uncomfortably from one foot to another. He's wearing black shirt and trousers underneath his kutte, and I expect he'll be going to the funeral.

"You gonna invite me in or just stand there staring?" he asks.

"What do you want?" I don't have the time or patience to deal with him if he's come to be an arse again.

"I heard you had the baby. I wanted to come sooner, but Cooper sent me on a run. How are you, Harper?" His face looks genuinely concerned and so, with a sigh, I open the door wider, indicating for him to come inside.

I watch as he peers into the basket and his face breaks into a smile. "Harper, she's so tiny." He reaches in and gently lifts her to his chest, cradling her against him like a pro. I feel a pang of jealousy—I don't feel that confident with my mothering skills just yet, but Marshall seems so at ease. "I have lots of siblings," he explains like he's read my mind.

"Are you going to the funeral?" I ask, pointing to his clothes. Marshall nods and then lowers himself onto the couch.

"Aren't you?"

"I thought about it, but maybe Kain will see it as insulting, seeing as Ginger and I didn't see eye to eye. Mila thinks it's not a good idea."

"Personally, I think Kain will appreciate the gesture, and honestly, he isn't coping too well right now. Maybe he needs to see a familiar face that he has an emotional connection with?"

"Since when did you care about Kain?" I ask with a laugh.

"I was being a selfish arse before. He loves you in his own way, and I shouldn't have stepped in on that." I frown. Marshall is acting weird, and when he catches me staring, he shrugs his shoulders. "I met someone." A smile forms on my lips. That explains his understanding behaviour. I'm genuinely happy for him. "I get it now, when you feel so strongly for someone and there's a threat, I get why he behaved like he did with me. It's just how I feel about Neve."

"Wow, so you didn't feel that about me?" I place a hand over my heart and fake pain.

Marshall laughs. "It ain't like that. It was different between us. We were hooking up and I fancied you, still do, but with Neve, it's different. I haven't even been there yet. That girl is making me work for it." I like the sound of her already because any girl who can make Marshall wait has to be special. "Anyway, I want you to meet her. I've told her all about you. I miss having you around, Harper. We were friends and I miss that."

I lean forward from my seat on the couch and reach for his knee. Placing a gentle squeeze there, I smile. "I've missed you too, and I can't wait to meet Neve."

"Why don't you come to the funeral, Harper? Let's get Kain back on his feet together, starting with him seeing that you're still here to support him no matter what."

"I'm not sure that's a good idea. Maybe Mila was right." The reality of me having to go and face him has me changing my mind. Besides, he never replied to my text of Willow's picture and that's evidence enough.

"You don't have to see him or approach him. Sit at the back. He just needs to know you're there for him, and the rest will come naturally."

When he sees that I'm still hesitant, he takes my hand. "I'll stay with you."

Kain

My chest feels heavy. I'm lying on my back, staring up at the blue sky while the baby sleeps in his pushchair next to me. I still haven't got a name. The ol' ladies are giving me shit, but I'm quite happy to refer to him as 'the baby' for now. I need to bury his mother today, in just over half an hour. Maybe after that, I'll think of a name, but right now, I need to take one day at a time.

I'm thankful for Cooper. He's arranged everything for today while I've spent my days holed up in my room with the baby and my nights screwing different club whores in my bathroom or the hall or anywhere near my room so I can still hear if the baby wakes up.

The black tie I'm wearing is restricting and uncomfortable, but Mila told me it was a necessity. That's bullshit, of course, because Ginger wasn't the suited and booted type of girl and she'd be laughing at me right now. Well, the old Ginger would have. The new Ginger, the one I'd become accustomed to seeing, probably would have sneered at me. I shake the image away.

A squawking sound comes from the pushchair, and I sit up. The baby doesn't often cry, only occasionally if he wants some attention, but the rest of the time, he's laidback. My mind wanders to Harper and her daughter. She texted me yesterday with a photograph and my first thought was how much she looks like Harper. She named her Willow, something we hadn't discussed, but then I didn't attend scans and appointments, so maybe I'd lost that right.

I lift the baby to me, and he immediately settles down as I place him against my chest. I've had to become an expert quickly.

"I guess we'd better go and say goodbye to your mumma, little man." I stand, keeping him to my chest as I guide the pushchair back towards the clubhouse. "I bet Aunty Mila is losing her shit right now."

I'm right, and the minute I walk in, Mila spins to me and sighs, relief flooding her features. "The car will be here any minute," she says, and I nod. I hadn't forgotten, but I needed a minute away from the madness of it all. I feel ready now, ready to say goodbye.

The cars arrive minutes later—one large black limousine to take me, Cooper, and Mila, and the hearse in front with Ginger. I take in the beautiful flowers that surround her solid white oak coffin. Large white lilies lay on the top, arranged perfectly. One side of the coffin has the word 'Mummy' in pink flowers and on the other is 'Virginia' in white and pink flowers. I don't know if Ginger liked flowers or what her favourite flowers were. It's one of the many things I never asked her, partly because I don't do romance and asking would have been pointless because I wouldn't have bothered to buy any, and secondly, because we didn't have those moments where we laid in bed chatting. We fucked, we had fun, and then she got sick, and so the talking part never really came.

We make the short way to the church. Lots of Hammers brothers are already waiting for our arrival, all in black and looking solemn. I know they're all here for me because many of them didn't care for Ginger. As the car comes to a stop, I spot her, right at the back, and I inhale painfully. I didn't expect to see her here and I'm not sure how to feel. I turn to Mila, who is cooing at the baby.

"What the fuck is she doing here?" The venom in my voice surprises me, and when Mila whips her head up to me, I can see that she's surprised too.

"I told her not to come, Kain, I swear. I didn't know about this." Her eyes are wide, and I know she's telling the truth.

"Watch the baby," I grate out.

Cooper takes my arm, halting me. "Is that a good idea, brother?" When I hesitate, he releases my arm. "I'm sure she's just here to show her support, and going out there screaming at her when you're already feeling shit, it won't end well. Concentrate on Ginger today, and you can sort the rest out tomorrow."

I know Cooper is right. I'll lose my shit and take out my feelings on Harper. I nod once, and Cooper pats me on the back. As I get out of the vehicle, I make sure not to look in her direction. My cold indifference should keep her away from me.

The service is nice as far as funerals go. Nice words are said from the few girls who she spoke to at the club. We listen to a prayer from the priest, and I mime to the hymns. After the service, I shake hands and kiss cheeks, nodding in all the right places. I chose to cremate Ginger. I didn't know what her wishes were, but I figured I could keep her ashes for our son, and he can scatter them when he's old enough to make that choice, or keep them, or whatever.

The line of mourners keeps moving past me as each person stops to say a few words. I stare blankly, feeling like a fraud. I didn't love Ginger, but I should have, and the guilt I feel from that now breaks me. And on top of that, the guilt from her illness weighs heavily on my shoulders.

Marshall stops in front of me and shakes my hand. "How are you holding up, man?" he asks.

"I've been asked that question so many times today that I'm not sure what the answer should be anymore." I glance to his left and my eyes freeze on Harper. She offers a small smile, which I don't return. "I asked her to come, Kain. I thought it would help to know that everyone is here for you."

"Some people I'm better off without," I say coldly. "And where's the kid?" That question falls from my lips before I have chance to stop it. I look Harper over, seeing that she looks well, considering she gave birth a few days ago.

"Gloria," she says, her voice wavering slightly.

"Then get back to her. You shouldn't leave her this soon after giving birth." I know I'm being cold, and it's intentional because I don't want her here. It feels wrong, and Ginger wouldn't have wanted her to come and fake sadness.

"Don't you want to see her? Aren't you just a little curious?" The sadness in her eyes almost breaks me, but I stand strong. I point to where Mila is standing holding my son, and Harper follows my direction.

"That's my priority right now. He's lost his mum, thanks to you. Now, get the fuck outta my sight." The line of her jaw tightens and tears fill her eyes. Marshall shakes his head in disappointment before following Harper, throwing his arm around her shoulders and leading her away.

I'm drunk. No, I'm past drunk. My bleary eyes try to focus on where Mila sits cradling my son, but it's no good. There're too many of them to pick just one and focus. My head falls against the back of the couch and I let out a groan. Why did I treat Harper like that today? Of course, I'm curious about my daughter. I want to know if she cries the same as her brother or if she's just as laidback as he is. I push myself to stand, taking a second to find my balance. Cooper rushes to my side, laughing. "Whoa, there, big guy, what's the rush?"

"I need to see her," I slur. I grab hold of Cooper's shoulder and lean closer. "Willow."

"I don't think that's a good idea tonight, Kain. Go tomorrow, when you've cleared your head." That comes from Mila, but I can't think of a better time, and so I move on wobbly legs towards the door. I know Cooper follows me, as I can hear the scuff of his heavy boots.

"Mila's right, brother."

"I'm seeing her now." I push out into the carpark and the fresh air hits me, which does nothing for my spinning head. I grab onto the wall to steady myself.

"Let me take you, Kain. You can't walk. You'll never make it." Before I know it, I'm in Cooper's car on the way to meet my daughter. I rest my head against the cool of the glass window and smile to myself. I'm excited to be meeting her.

CHAPTER FIFTEEN

Harper

I open the front door and stare into the face of Cooper, who looks self-assured and arrogant. It's a look he often has when he's doing something he doesn't agree with but feels he has no choice. It was the look he had the day he stood Mila up at their first wedding attempt.

"How can I help you, Mr. President?" I ask with a cheeky smile. It's taken me a long time to accept Cooper. The way he treated my best friend was unforgivable, and it's only recently that I've felt I can tease him and throw banter his way, despite him being my boss for over a year. He looks back out onto the road where his car is parked and then back to me.

"Kain's in the truck. He's asleep, but he wanted to come and meet Willow." I'm confused by the sudden change of heart and my face must show it because he feels the need to explain further. "He's drunk. The funeral hit him pretty hard today."

"Then I suggest you turn the car around and take his drunken arse home. He can meet Willow when he's sober." I try to close the door, but he shoves a boot in the way and I roll my eyes. There's no way Cooper's going to talk me into seeing Kain while he's drunk. "I get it, okay, but if I take him home now, when he wakes, he's probably gonna jump on his bike and come here himself. I don't want that on my conscience."

"He can't see her if he's drunk, Cooper. How can you even suggest I let him?"

"Can he at least come in and sleep it off?"

I can't have Kain here. I'm far too weak for him, despite how he's been towards me, and if he wakes and rushes out of here, regretting his drunken decision, my heart won't be able to take it. I shake my head. "I'm sorry, it's just not a good idea." This time, he lets me close the door. I lock it and use the deadbolt for extra security.

I go to bed, deciding to get as much sleep as Willow will allow. She cries non-stop usually, so the fact that she's now asleep in her cot next to my bed is a chance I can't afford to miss. I'm asleep before my head fully hits the pillow.

It's a terrible night as Willow wakes several times for a feed. Sometimes, I'm convinced she just wants to suckle on me for comfort, which most people might find cute, but I'm too exhausted, and by the time morning comes around, I just want to sit and cry. I made plans for my father and Gloria to visit with me this morning and then for my mother and father to visit in the afternoon. It makes me tired just thinking of seeing them, but I shower and dress quickly, all while Willow screams her lungs out. As I head downstairs, there's a banging on the door. I sigh because it's far too early for my father. I use the spy hole and groan out loud. A tired and pissed-off looking Kain stands with his hands on his hips.

"Good morning," I say, opening for him to enter.

"You know I slept on your doorstep, right?" he snaps, still waiting in the doorway.

"Make it quick, Kain. I'm expecting visitors today."

"Are you shitting me? I'm not rushing when I'm here to meet my daughter."

"Well, then, you should have arranged it better rather than turning up at night drunk." I watch as he steps into the living room, closing my front door hard. Willow screams louder, and I try to hold her to me so she calms, but she fights me and I sigh. "She cries non-stop. I feel like she hates me."

Kain holds out his arms until I hand her to him. He holds her to his leather-clad chest, and gently rests her bottom in his large hand. He makes shushing noises, and she stops screaming. I know he meant it to help, but it just makes me feel even more useless.

"She smells delicious," he comments, his nose against her soft willowy hair. I curl up on the couch and smile as I watch him gently swaying. He knows how to take care of her and that settles me. I feel my eyes grow heavy.

"Harper." The sound of my name comes again, and I open one eye. Kain is staring at me, Willow in his arms. "Your father is here." I dive into sitting position, almost hitting Kain's head with my own. There's a loud knock at the door and Kain heads towards it before my words and brain catch up.

My father stares at Kain and then looks down to the bundle in his arms. "Harper was just catching up on some sleep. Come on in."

I watch my father and Gloria step inside. Gloria instantly smiles at the bundle in Kain's arms, and he offers Willow to her. Even though she met her yesterday while she took care of her so I could attend Ginger's funeral, she still looks amazed.

"And you are?" asks my father, glaring at Kain.

"He's Cooper's friend. He was helping me out," I jump in before Kain can answer. Kain looks to me with disappointment and my eyes plead with him not to say anything.

"Why is he helping? Where's her father?"

"I am her father," grits out Kain. "Kain." He holds his hand out for my father to shake, but he just stares down at it with distain. My heart trembles and I place a hand to my chest like that will somehow magically slow it down. My father turns to me, his eyebrows almost meeting his hairline.

"Harper?" he asks. I don't trust words right now, so I nod.

"You promised me it wasn't a biker," he snaps.

"Because I knew how you'd be. We aren't together or anything, it was an accident." When they all stare at me with shocked expressions, I backtrack. "A happy accident, obviously."

"I'm gonna leave you to discuss this. I'll be over later with the baby so he can meet Willow," Kain says, then leaves. I groan and close my eyes, and my father's eyes almost bug out of his head. The news that Willow has a half-brother is going to make everything so much worse.

Gloria takes a seat and smiles down at Willow. "Michael, come and sit down. Take a look at your granddaughter. Save the drama for another time."

My father's face is exasperated as he glares between the two of us. "Are we just going to ignore the fact that she's given birth to a gang member's child?" I want to remind him of the secrets he holds from Gloria and my mother, but I bite my tongue.

My father sits and glances over Willow before sighing and taking her from Gloria. I'm surprised by the action because I know that when I was growing up, he wasn't a loving kind of father. My mum did all the nappy changes and feeds until she got bored of being tied to me while my father travelled, and she hired a nanny. He was much better when the twins were born. Libby and Bella held a special place in his heart, and I often wonder if he resented me and my mother and that, in fact, he was always supposed to meet Gloria and have the twins. He made it no secret that he didn't want my mum to go ahead with her pregnancy.

"Doesn't it make you broody?" gushes Gloria as she rises to her feet. "Let me make us all a drink." I watch her retreat into the kitchen and then I scowl at my father.

"Have you sorted things with Anton?" I hiss.

"About that," he begins, and my eyes widen. That means he's about to let me down again and reveal he hasn't spoken to Anton or sorted anything. "He's off the radar."

"What do you mean?" I whisper, my voice almost at a screech.

"We haven't heard from him for almost a week now. Gloria's tried, and I've left him messages, but he hasn't replied. Gloria wants to call the police, but I'm glad he's out of the picture and so I keep putting her off."

"Oh my god, what if he's hurt? If he's missing, you have to report it to the police." I don't know why I'm defending Anton, but something doesn't feel right and leaving him as missing is not the answer as much as my father feels it is. I often wonder how far my father would go to cover up his lies and keep living the best of both worlds.

"Keep your nose out. I'm doing this my way."

I press my mouth into a hard line as Gloria reappears with a tray of coffees. The truth must come out sooner or later. I decide to weigh up my mother's state of mind later to see if she appears strong enough to handle the truth.

By the afternoon, I'm tired and cranky. Willow genuinely appears to hate me, as she settles lovely when anyone else holds her and screams when I try. The only time she stops for me is if I cram my boob in her mouth and she feeds.

My father returns, this time with my mother, and I laugh at the absurdity of the situation. If it goes on forever, will I have to get Willow to lie too? Having two grandmothers is going to confuse her, and if she is anything like Kain, she'll talk straight and without fear of consequence. My mother looks tired and pale. Her usual makeup is in place and her hair is styled professionally from her daily trips to the salon, but she seems on edge.

"Would you like to take her?" I offer, but she shakes her head. She isn't one to coo over babies, and apparently, that even applies to her first granddaughter. "Is everything okay?"

"What are you trying to ask, Harper?" my father butts in.

"If she's okay. She appears off." I glare at him, letting him know not to piss me off right now because I'm a hormonal mess and his luck is running out.

"I'm fine, Harper. Just tired," she says, adding a little smile for my reassurance.

"I was thinking, why don't you stay here with me for a few days? I could use the help with Willow."

"Because you're a single mum?" asks my father snidely. My mother's back stiffens and she looks to me for answers. It's funny that she never questions how my father knows this stuff.

"I'm not exactly single. Kain will be around for Willow, we just aren't together. It happens all the time, and co-parenting's quite common these days." I'm defensive because although I might be shitting myself about the whole single mum status, I don't want anyone to know. I want them to think I'm holding it all together despite not combing my hair out after my shower or brushing my teeth.

"I have plans, Harper. Maybe another time." I knew she'd say no, but it still hurts me to hear it out loud. She doesn't get that there won't be another time because Willow will grow and I won't ever get this time back. Willow begins to cry again and, quite honestly, I want to join her.

"I have to feed her," I say, and my father stands abruptly, seeing this as his chance to leave.

CHAPTER SIXTEEN

Harper

My parents have been gone almost an hour when Kain returns. I can tell by his stony expression that he's pissed with me. He carries his son against his chest and it's hard not to feel a little warmth at how good he looks holding a baby. As usual, Willow is crying and so he lays his son down in the crib and takes her from me. As predicted, she stops squawking, and I sigh with exasperation. "How do you do that?"

"I'm a natural," he mutters, taking a seat. I peer into the crib at the sleeping boy. He's gorgeous, and it's hard to tell who he looks like most with him being so small, but he's definitely one of those kinds of babies everyone coos over because he's so perfect.

"Have you got a name for him?" I ask, not taking my eyes from his sleeping face.

"Nope." I glance over to Kain, his expression still unfriendly and cold. I sigh and go back to baby watching. I wish Willow was content.

"Are you struggling with Willow?" he asks, and I whip back to look at him.

"No, why would you say that?" I gasp. It's one thing for me to think it but another to admit it out loud.

"I'm just asking. Don't get all defensive. I know she cries a lot, and you look tired." I subconsciously smooth over my unbrushed hair, feeling the sting of his words. "I read online that you should be taking it easy because of the C-section."

"I am taking it easy." I stand and wince when my stitches pull. "I'm doing just fine on my own." I go to the kitchen and turn on the coffee pot. How dare he come here and question my parenting? He's been in Willow's life less than twenty-four hours. I spoon sweetener into the mugs with some force, dropping the spoon into one and folding my arms across my chest. Kain might have the knack with Willow, but Mila told me that she'd read that babies settle with others over their breastfeeding mother because they can smell the milk. When it's just me and Willow, all she wants is to feed, and when I don't feed her, she cries.

"You wanna slam around in here a little louder so you can wake the babies?" His familiar growl makes me jump in fright. "Why didn't you tell your parents about me?"

"And say what? That I've gone and gotten myself pregnant by a man who already has a pregnant girlfriend. I didn't want to give my father any more reasons to hate me."

Kain takes a seat at the dinner table. "I haven't opened her letter." He sighs, and when his eyes reach mine, they're filled with pain. It reminds me of his loss and that he's grieving for Ginger.

"She gave it to me after she told me that she'd lied to the cops about you. What happened, Kain?" I place his coffee on the table and take a seat opposite him. "She said that she'd hit you. Is that what all the cuts and bruises were?"

Kain stares at me for a short time like he's assessing whether to tell me, and then he sighs again and takes a drink of his coffee. "Why does your father hate you?"

"He's cheating on my mother." I figure that if I want him to open up, then I need to open up first. It's no secret that these MC guys don't talk about their feelings. "When I was just a little girl, I woke one night and went into my parents' bedroom. My father was in there with another woman, Gloria. At the time, my mother was in a hospital. She's not been well in her head for a long time." Something changes in his eyes, and I feel able to continue. It feels good to say all of this out loud. "I don't remember much about what I said, but I know it made my father cross. He said that if I told anyone, then my mother would never be able to come home ever again. I was just a kid and I wanted her home."

I pause, trying to remember why I wanted that because it's not like she was ever maternal towards me. "After that, I saw Gloria regularly. She didn't know about my mother . . . well, not completely. To this day, she thinks my mother is locked up in a hospital for people with mental illness. My father takes my mother away with him on business trips most of the time, and on the days that he wants to see Gloria, he sends my mother on spa breaks or tells her lies so he can get away for a few days."

"And so, you've had to lie to both of them?" Kain looks surprised and almost sympathetic.

"That's why I have the money in the bank. I mean, he never said that's what it was for, but I know it's hush money."

"Why don't you tell them? You're older now, he can't threaten you."

"No, but he threatens my mother. He will pay to have her locked away in a mental institute. He knows people in high places, and honestly, she isn't well. She takes anti-depressant medicine and some other stuff, and when she questions my father, he gets her personal carer to mess with her meds. It can set her off for days. He says the carer is on his payroll and he'll back my father up when it comes to reports on my mother's behaviour." As the words leave me, I feel my shoulders lift slightly. It all sounds so bizarre and farfetched, but Kain is from a world of corruption and so I know he'll get it.

We stay silent for a few beats and then he presses his lips into a firm line before eventually saying, "Ginger wasn't well either. The day you saw her screaming, well, that'd been going on for some time." I'd thought as much, but I don't interrupt him now that's he's finally opening up. "When I met Ginger, she was just a hang-on to the club and all I saw was her flaming hair and big eyes. I was hooked." His truth hurts, but I keep my face neutral. I can't be jealous over a dead woman. "The other guys warned me, said she was a little crazy sometimes, but I wasn't gonna let that put me off, so I pursued her. All I wanted was a hook-up." *Much like me*, I think to myself.

A newborn cry rings out and Kain rises gracefully from the table, considering his size. He goes to the living room, returning a minute later with his son. "I laid them together, and Willow settled straight next to him." His gruff voice almost sounds emotional. He places a change bag on the table and rummages inside, producing a bottle with some powdered milk in the bottom. He uses the water from the kettle to make it up and then holds it under the tap to cool it. I smile in admiration at how at ease Kain is with his new-found fatherhood.

"So," he continues from across the kitchen, "Ginger and I hook up, more than once, and then she just disappears. That happens a few times. I don't mind much, and I move on to you." He grins at me like he's pictured the memory of us in his head. "We have fun and then, without warning, Ginger turns back up and tells me she's pregnant. She tells me straight that because of that, she needs to stop taking her crazy meds, and so she passes that to me. Do I want this kid? Will I stick by her if she sacrifices her mental well-being for my kid? And what was I supposed to say to all of that? The thought of having a kid didn't scare the shit outta me, and so I told her, yeah, keep the kid, I'll stick by her and support her." He pauses again and checks the temperature of the bottled milk. He smiles down at the bundle in his arms and then sticks the bottle in his mouth.

"This kid's gonna be big and strong, he drinks so much milk." Kain sits back across from me, all the while staring down at the baby. "I was trying do the right thing. It killed me, Harper, because by then, I liked you. Your crazy games to get my attention had won and it was too hard to give you up, so I had the best of both worlds. By day, I was fucking you any place I could get you, and by night, I was fucking Ginger in our bed, in our home." He lets the words settle between us before looking me in the eye. I hold his stare, wanting him to see the pain he's caused me by admitting that. I suspected, but when he was with me and I tried to tell him no, when I tried to make him do the right thing and go back to Ginger, he would tell me they weren't like that, that it was just complicated. Back then, it was more about the fucking rather than the talking.

"You lied to me," I whisper, and he nods, seemingly unfazed by the hurt in my voice.

"And then you came at me telling me you were pregnant and my world stopped. I had Ginger depending on me. Her mental health was slipping fast, and she needed me to anchor her. You were so fiercely independent. There was no expectation from you, and you told me straight that you didn't want me to leave Ginger for you . . ." He trails off. I told him that because I didn't want to put him in a position where he felt he had to choose. Looking back, I'm not sure if that was because I was scared he'd choose her, so I made that choice for us both.

"These last few months with Ginger have been . . . trying. She'd lose her shit and hit out at me or hit herself in the stomach. She blamed me, and I don't fault her for that. I should never have made that decision. Her mental well-being should have been the priority." There's regret in his words and I smile sympathetically.

"Ginger wasn't well. She knew the risks when she stopped the medication. You can't take anything that she said in those last few months personally, Kain."

"Well, I do. I blame us both, me and you." My mouth falls open in shock. "We shouldn't have carried on the affair. You shouldn't have told her about the baby. Damn it, every time I think of that moment, I want to walk away and never see you again."

"You started the affair in the first place. I didn't know you were sleeping with us both in the beginning, and you did that knowing she was pregnant. I didn't know she wasn't well, but you did. You should have told me. When she asked me if the baby was yours, I didn't want to lie anymore."

"Why?" He stops and then sighs. "You lied since being a kid to your mum."

His words cut me deep. I'd confided that information to him and now he's using it against me. "Low fucking blow, Kain," I mutter, leaving the room.

CHAPTER SEVENTEEN

Kain

I feel like a shit. It's like my brain finds the most brutal way to hurt her and I just say the words and watch the pain. Deep down, I know I'm more to blame for Ginger. But Harper confessing about Willow was the final straw for her, and I can't get her face out my mind whenever I think back to that moment. It plays over and over like it's on a damn loop and it breaks me to know that she killed herself right after learning the truth.

I finish feeding the baby and then go into the living room. "Let's go and grab some dinner."

Harper looks at me like I've lost my mind, and maybe I have, but deep down, I need this to work. I want to see my daughter and I have to think about what will happen to this kid if I get sent back inside. He will need a mother, and seeing as Harper's already had my kid, I want her help, she owes Ginger that much. "Get dressed and brush your damn hair. I'm hungry." She looks exhausted, but instead of arguing, she does as I ask her without a fuss.

When she returns wearing a simple summer dress with her hair brushed and tied up in a messy bun on her head, I smile. She's looking more like the Harper I know.

We go to a diner just a few streets away. Harper looks on edge, constantly peeking into the car seat at Willow and fussing with her blankets, and I wonder if this is the first time she's been out of the house since the birth. We settle into a booth, so we have enough room to accommodate the car seats with the babies. A pretty waitress comes across immediately, smiling radiantly at me. She glances over Harper and then takes in the two babies. "Wow, twins," she says, giving the babies that look all women do whenever they see something cute.

"No, not twins," says Harper with a steely edge to her tone. The waitress looks confused but shrugs her shoulders and turns back to me for our order.

I order us each a burger and fries, much to Harper's irritation. She always hated it when I ordered for her, and so I often did it just to annoy her. Today, it's out of convenience. She needs to get back home to rest. We eat in silence and then Willow wakes and begins crying. Harper looks alarmed and glances around at the other tables. "What's wrong?" I ask.

"It's packed out in here and she needs feeding."

"Then feed her," I say with a shrug.

"I can't feed her in here with all these people. Take me home, Kain." I look around, it's busy, but I don't understand why she wouldn't want to feed our daughter in here when everyone else is eating just fine. "Kain, I don't want to attract attention."

"Jesus, woman, you can't even see anything when you're feeding her. Trust me, I've looked." Harper almost smiles until she remembers what I'm asking her to do. "Harper, feed my daughter." I use my stern voice and see her waver.

She reaches for Willow and turns away from the neighbouring tables. She fiddles around with her top and then places a blanket around Willow so they're both suitably covered. "That wasn't so hard, was it?"

We get back to Harper's and I hover in the doorway. I should get going, but I've enjoyed hanging out today and a part of me doesn't want it to end. She watches me from inside, waiting for me to say something. "I should go," I eventually say.

"Club girls waiting for you?" she asks, and I mentally curse Mila for opening her gossiping mouth.

"Something like that," I say, and she nods, her face going back to that stony expression she often gives when I've said something she hates. "Have you met anyone?" I don't know why I asked because in my head I warned myself not to say it out loud.

Harper laughs. It's throaty and all Harper, and I miss that sound. "Would you be attracted to a woman who's just had a C-section?" She lays Willow in the basket. "Not forgetting the fact that I can't have sex right now, thanks to this little lady, or the fact she's permanently attached to me, feeding."

I smirk, thankful to Willow for putting her mum out of action. "Can we meet up again tomorrow?"

Harper chews on her lower lip. "Wouldn't you prefer some time alone with Willow? It's been really nice spending time with you and the baby, but eventually, you'll want time alone with her."

"She's too young to be away from you, and with her breastfeeding, it's just easier. I'm up before the judge on Monday. I'd like you to get to know the baby before then."

"Why?" she asks. I step inside and close the door. I wasn't going to mention it, but now that I've put it out there, I may as well finish.

"I want you to take care of him if I go back inside."

Harper laughs but stops when she sees I'm deadly serious. "Oh my god, is that what this has been about?"

"No, of course, not. I mean, I wanted to ask you, so I needed to see you, but I've had a nice time today." Harper watches me sceptically. "I know it's a big ask, but Willow is his only family now."

"Nice," mutters Harper angrily. "Throw that in to make me feel bad. Are you likely to go back inside?" There's no point in me lying to her, so I nod. Joanne thinks I'm looking at five years max.

"I need to sleep on this, Kain. Yah know, I thought it was odd when you had a complete behaviour transplant. One minute, you can't stand to look at me, and the next, you wanna hang out. For a minute there, I thought you actually gave a crap about us."

I reach across to her and stroke a thumb down her cheek. I place a careful and gentle kiss there. "You know I wouldn't ask unless I was desperate. The club would help, but he needs a mum, and you're already doing it for his sister. It makes sense."

"None of it makes sense, Kain. You hate me, but you want me to raise your son."

"I don't hate you. I'm struggling with what you did and the way things turned out, but I don't hate you."

"You blame me."

I remain silent, unable to answer her honestly. "Just think about it. Please."

Back at the clubhouse, there's a party. Not for anything specific, but just because sometimes these nights get like this and everyone needs to let off steam. Mila offers to take the baby upstairs because she's tired, her pregnancy taking its toll on her.

Cooper slaps me hard on the back in greeting, and then Tanner joins us, looking miserable. "Brother, you always look pissed with the world lately. What's going on?" I ask. Cooper and Tanner exchange a look. "Hey, I might not be the VP at the moment, but I still get to know shit," I snap. I've let Marshall keep the temporary title of Vice President for now, but I intend to take that right back once the court case is out the way.

"Things aren't great between me and Brook lately," mutters Tanner. I can't hide the shock on my face because those two are solid. He met her one time and then stalked her until she agreed to go out with him, and I'm pretty sure he hasn't left her side since. We often question how she puts up with his crazy because he's so intense yet she's cute and fun.

"Shit, I wasn't expecting that." Thinking about it, I guess it is odd that she isn't somewhere in this room right now. He's always just a reach away from her side.

"We found out that she can't have kids," he mutters, and I wince. It's no secret that Brook wants to be a mum. It's all she's talked about, and Tanner put it off because he can't bear to share her. "She's taken it real hard. She doesn't even want me in the same room as her right now."

"Give her time, brother. Things will get easier," Cooper reassures him. I'm not convinced Tanner has the patience to give her time. Watching him now is painful, he looks so lost without her. I pat his shoulder because I have no comforting words to offer him right now.

"How did it go with Harper?" asks Cooper.

"Good, I think. I asked if she'd have the kid if things go bad on Monday."

"We'll all help her. That kid is part of this club." It means a lot. The brotherhood is one of the most important things to me, and if I go back inside, I'll miss this. "Did you open the letter yet?" he asks, and I shake my head. When Mila handed it to me, it was a shock. Ginger wasn't one for words or soppy love notes, and so whatever is in that letter is going to rock my world again and I'm not strong enough.

"What if it's good news?" asks Tanner thoughtfully.

"Like what?" I ask with a head shake. There was no good news that Ginger could possibly put in a letter unless it was to tell me this was all one big joke and she was alive after all.

"Maybe it's a name for that poor kid you keep calling 'the baby'?" he suggests. That makes sense.

I pull it from my pocket. It's crumpled, so I straighten it out the best I can. "Are you gonna open it now?" Tanner almost looks excited, and I feel bad that the guy's enjoying the mystery of a letter from a dead woman way more than he should be. I take a deep breath and tear the envelope. I open it out and begin to read it to myself. Within seconds, I'm smiling.

Kain,

First of all, I want to apologise. I'm sure the last few months have been hell for you, and I won't have made your life easy. But please know, it's not intentional. I made the choice to die way before any of this. When I found out I was pregnant, I had to give you a choice. And it's not fair one, because I'm not giving you the full facts. But I can't. Because I can't risk you changing my mind about my plan to die. I'm tired, Kain. So very tired. This illness has taken my life, and I know you'll never truly understand why I had to leave, especially after giving you the greatest gift I could. But life isn't for everyone, and I choose to stop the circus in my head before I hurt someone. So, take care of our baby boy, and although I have no real right, the name I would have chosen to call him would be Kian. It's a play on the letters of yours and my late brother's name.

I'm sorry I couldn't stay for you both, but I know you'll do right by him. I love you both very much.

Attached is a second letter addressed to the police.

I, Virginia Shaw, lied. Kain Morgan never laid a finger on me, and he never would. In fact, it's been quite the opposite and he was too polite to speak up. He's never hit me. On the day the police called in, I smashed up our home and I hit Kain. I was too ashamed to tell the truth. I'm sorry. I hope he forgives me.

I smile, relief washing over me, and pass the letter to Cooper. He scans it, also breaking into a smile. He pulls out his mobile phone and dials a number, pressing the device to his ear. "Yes, I know what the goddamn time is. Listen up, I've got something to help with Kain's case."

CHAPTER EIGHTEEN

Harper

It's been a few days since I saw Kain, and I've heard nothing. Typical he'd drop something so huge on me and then disappear. And now, it's Monday evening and Kain had court today. I've tried calling him and Mila, but neither have answered and my mind is running overtime. What if he's back in prison? What if I have to bring two babies up? I spent the entire weekend thinking about it, and he's right, it makes sense to take in Willow's brother. After all, I'm one of the reasons his mother isn't around anymore, and I know the club would help.

I glance at my watch again, seeing it's almost eight in the evening. Someone would know something by now, and so I decide to head to the clubhouse to find out for myself. I'm not supposed to be driving so soon after my C-section, but I decide to risk it. I have to know the outcome.

I stop the car outside the clubhouse. The gates were open, and music can be heard even from outside. I guess there's a party, which would mean one of two things—either Kain has walked free, or he went back inside and Cooper's trying to keep the brothers' spirits up. I take Willow from her seat and head inside.

It's real busy, but I spot Jase first and tap him on the shoulder. "Hey, Harper, glad you could make it. How's things?" he shouts over the music.

"Good. What's the party for?"

"Kain, all charges dropped." Jase smiles wide. "He's somewhere around here if you wanna congratulate him, but the last time I saw him, he was being congratulated by the new club arse." I offer a tight smile and watch as he saunters off into the crowd. I can't believe I've spent the day worrying for him and he's been back here celebrating without a second thought for me.

I'm about to leave when I hear my name being called. Looking around, I spot Brook waving frantically at me. I wait for her to push through a few people before she's standing before me. "Am I glad to see you," she huffs. "Come on." She takes my hand and pulls me towards the clubhouse. Once inside the main room, she closes the conjoining bar door, shutting out the loud noise.

"Actually, Brook, I was just about to leave."

"Oh, sorry, I thought you got my message," she says. There's something on her mind, she's fidgeting, and when I shake my head, she sighs. "I texted you like five minutes ago to ask if I could come over to see you."

"I was probably driving. I came to see what had happened at the courthouse today, but I guess that's obvious by the party. Why'd yah wanna come over? Are you okay?"

"Not really. I need space from Tanner." I try to hide the shock. Brook and Tanner are inseparable, and if he finds out she's trying to get space, he may well lock her in his room.

"You guys have fallen out?" I ask.

"No, well, sort of. I just need some me time, yah know?" I nod, knowing what it's like to need head space from these overbearing Hammers men.

"That's fine. You can come back with me, I have the car out front. Before we leave though, is Mila around?"

"No, she took Asher to her mum's, and she isn't back yet. Cooper is screwing." The door opens and Kain falls through it, laughing and holding the hand of a pretty brunette. He doesn't see us until he's fallen onto the couch and has the girl straddling him. When he spots me, he scrambles to sit up, moving the girl from his lap and sitting her beside him.

"Harper, what are you doing here?" he asks, shock clear on his face.

"Nothing much. I was just leaving," I say, forcing a tight smile. It shouldn't bother me that he's with a woman, but it really does. Today could have been huge, life-changing for all of us, and yet he didn't have the decency to call and let me know he was okay, that he didn't need me to raise his son for the next five years. It's clear his visit the other day was purely to soften me up so that he had a mother for his child should the worst happen, and now that he doesn't need me, he's here, fucking about with club girls.

"Well, stay, have a drink. Let me see Willow." He's wobbly when he stands, so I pull Willow closer to my chest. He frowns. "I've only had a couple. I'm celebrating," he defends.

"Congratulations. Nice of you to let me know the outcome today, thanks." I turn back to Brook. "Let's go."

"Wait, Harper," shouts Kain, running after us. He takes my arm, slowing me down. "Harper, please, let me see Willow for five minutes. I should have called, I'm sorry. It was chaos today."

"Call me to schedule a visit and you can take her for a few hours. I'm trying to bottle feed her to make it easier for you," I say, pulling free of his hold.

"Schedule a visit? What the fuck does that mean?" he snaps.

"It means if you want to see her, then call me and we can sort that out. Go back to your club arse and your party," I say angrily. I leave before I burst into tears over him, yet again.

"Damn," says Brook as we get into my car. "I thought he was gonna explode back there . . ." Her words trail off, and I look up to see what shut her up. Tanner is moving towards the car, looking pissed. His fists are clenched, and his shoulders hunched. He looks scary when he's mad.

"Fuck," she mumbles.

"Did he know you were taking some time away?" I ask, and she shakes her head without breaking eye contact with him. "Shit, Brook, he's gonna freak out," I hiss.

"Then drive," she instructs, pulling on her belt quickly. I start the engine, but Tanner is too close, and he steps in front of the car, placing his hands on the bonnet. His eyes are burning into Brook and his nostrils flare with anger.

"Christ, he looks like a bull about to charge. Now, what do I do?" I ask.

"Reverse," she mutters.

"Are you sure, Brook, because—"

"Reverse!" she cuts in, this time louder. I slam my foot on the pedal and reverse out of the carpark and onto the main road, leaving him glaring after us.

"What the hell is going on?" I ask. "This isn't like you guys."

"We're working through some stuff," she mutters. "He doesn't understand that I just want some time alone. He can't give me space, and I need it so bad right now."

We turn onto my road, and I spot Mila and Asher immediately. They're sitting on my doorstep reading a book together. As I stop the car, they look up. "Two more stowaways," I say.

We all go inside, and Mila makes sure to lock the front door as well as deadbolt it. It only makes me more suspicious, and I wonder what the hell happened today. Willow is asleep from the car journey, so I lay her straight into her basket in the living room. I turn on the television for Asher and hand him the remote because he insists that he's a big boy and can find his own TV show. The girls head to the kitchen, and I follow, flicking on the kettle before joining them at the table.

"So," I start, looking between them, "what's going on?"

"I left Cooper," blurts Mila, and Brook and I turn to her in surprise. "He pulled me up because I was eating a tub of ice cream today. Who the fuck does he think he is? I might be piling on the pounds while he's working out every spare second of the day, but I'm pregnant and I needed sugar." She's almost growling, and I hide my laugh behind my hands. "He was all judgey, saying stuff about how extra baby weight is hard to lose."

I gasp because it was a little insensitive of him when she's so late on in her pregnancy. "Does he know you've left him?" I ask.

"Not yet. He thinks I'm at my mother's for the day. I was due home twenty minute ago."

"You know this is the first place he'll come looking," I point out, and then I turn to Brook. "And Tanner knows you're here, so he'll be here soon too."

"If he shows up yelling, I'm calling the cops. I need a night away, and he's gonna give it to me even if it means he's locked up in a cell."

"Are you gonna tell us what's happened?" asks Mila.

"I can't have kids," Brook blurts out. I'm truly shocked as I never expected that. "They've run some tests and I'm waiting on results to find the cause, but I can't have kids. Tanner doesn't care. He's relieved." She can't hide the devastation on her face.

"Did he say that?" asks Mila gently.

"No, but he's spent years telling me he doesn't want kids, making excuses, delaying it, and now I can't have them, so of course he's relieved. When they told us, he looked like a huge weight had been lifted." Brook bursts into tears, and we both rush to her side, wrapping her into a hug. "I wanted a baby so bad, a little girl that Tanner could protect and love. He never had that as a child, so he thinks he can't love a kid, but I wanted to show him that he could," she sobs.

"There are so many options, Brook. It doesn't mean you'll never be parents," I say.

NICOLA JANE

"After seeing the relief on his face, I know I'll never be a mother if I stay with him. That's why I need space, to work out what I want. I need to see how it feels to breathe without him being by my side."

"Does he know how you feel?" asks Mila, stroking hair from Brook's face.

"He doesn't ever want to talk about serious stuff. We fight, we fuck, and the rest of the time, he just watches me. It isn't normal, and I don't think I can do it anymore."

I get up to make us all a coffee. I can't imagine Brook without Tanner and vice versa. I'm not sure Tanner will survive without her. There's a bang on the door and we all freeze, our eyes darting to each other. It happens again, and this time, Willow begins to cry. I go to the living room and get her from her basket. I put the safety chain on the door and open it. Kain stands there looking drunk and tired. "What?" I ask.

"What's with the chain? Open the door."

"I have the girls here, Kain. What do you want?" I didn't expect to see him. In fact, I was sure he'd be buried inside the club girl right about now.

"To see Willow," he sighs and shrugs his huge shoulders, "and you, I guess."

"I'm always an afterthought for you, Kain. If I hadn't shown tonight, you wouldn't have even thought about me at all. Go home."

"That's not true, Harper. I don't want to think about you, but you're always in here," he growls, tapping his head. "I should hate you, but somehow, I can't stop thinking about you."

"You're drunk. Sleep it off." I sigh as Cooper's bike comes rumbling to a stop outside. "Mila, Cooper's here too," I shout back through to the kitchen.

"I don't want to see him," she replies. Great, now I have two big angry men to deal with.

"Harper, open the damn door. This is ridiculous," snaps Kain, trying to push against the door, but the chain holds strong. Cooper approaches, looking just as pissed as Kain.

"Is she here?" he demands to know.

"Of course, she's here, but she doesn't want to see you. What were you thinking? The girl can eat as much ice cream as she wants," I say with a smirk.

"Is that what all this is about, because I told her to be careful with what she eats?" he asks, looking genuinely surprised.

"Wow," slurs Kain, "you told a pregnant woman to watch her food intake?" He grins and shakes his head. "I thought I was dumb."

"Oh, right, cos you're on the right side of this door," says Cooper sarcastically, causing Kain's smile to fade.

"You should both go home. I also have Brook here, and I'm sure Tanner is cut up without her, so you can all be sad together."

"Is it like a witch gathering?" jokes Kain, and I scowl.

"Go home." I close the door and go back to the kitchen. "So, now what?"

"Girls' night?" suggests Mila with a smile.

CHAPTER NINETEEN

Kain

I roll over and hit something warm. Opening one eye, I'm face to face with Cooper. We both sit up in alarm and scramble apart. "What the hell?" I yell.

"Man, were you about to snuggle up to me?" he asks.

"No," I almost screech. We're on the floor of the main room in the clubhouse, and my body aches. I glance around and spot Tanner laying on one of the couches. I'm not sure why we didn't take that option. It's not like there aren't enough couches around here. "Why are we on the floor?" I croak.

"Not sure, brother, but it's not the strangest place I've woken," Cooper replies, with a laugh.

Tanner stretches out and rolls onto his back, revealing a very naked Melissa, one of the new girls who's been hanging around here. I exchange a shocked look with Cooper. "Tanner," I whisper hiss, and he groans, opening his eyes. I nod to Melissa, who's tucked into his side. "What the fuck, brother?"

He frowns and turns to his side. Then he moves so fast, she almost rolls off the couch. She sits, looking dazed for a second. Tanner grips his unfastened jeans. "What the fuck are you doing there?" he yells. "Did we . . . did I . . ." He trails off and buries his face in his hands. "FUCKKK," he yells.

"Relax, big guy, it was a bit of fun," says Melissa, rising gracefully from her position on the couch, not at all ashamed of being naked.

"You can't tell anyone about this," he snaps, glaring down at her. "I've got an ol' lady, and she'll kill us both."

Melissa chews on her lower lip and looks up at Tanner through her eyelashes. "I'm not gonna breathe a word to anyone, but you owe me," she says with a wink, and then she saunters from the room and heads for the stairs.

"You realise she's only nineteen, right?" Cooper asks, and Tanner lets out a roar like he's in some kind of physical pain.

"Man, I was so drunk, I don't know how the hell I got it up. Shit, fuck, shit," he rants, pacing back and forth.

"Look, the only people who know about this are us three and her. No one's gonna know, Tanner." I'm trying to reassure him, but for all we know, anyone could have walked through the main room while we were all passed out.

"I have to tell Brook. I've never cheated on her in my life, I love her," he groans. "Why would I do that?"

"Brother, you've been in turmoil these last few days. It was too much alcohol and a lack of Brook being here to ground you. We've all fucked up at one point or another," says Cooper.

"She's gonna leave my arse for this," he moans into his hands.

"Then don't tell her, brother. It was one mistake," I say, knowing mistakes can be so much worse if kept secret, but I can't stand to see the guy so cut up. And we all know how much he loves Brook. This was a genuine mistake, and the guy probably thought Melissa was Brook in his drunken state. "And if any of the other brothers have seen anything, they're not gonna breathe a word to anyone, so you're all good, man. Just don't say anything."

Tanner looks to Cooper, who shrugs and then nods in agreement. Eventually, he nods too and sighs. "Okay, I'm gonna shower and then I'm gonna get my ol' lady home where she belongs," he mutters.

Once Tanner's gone, Cooper lets out a long, low whistle. "Don't tell her, really, Kain?"

"Well, what did you want me to say, go tell her and watch your whole world implode? We both know he can't function without Brook. The feisty little fairy keeps him on his toes, and his obsession with her is not only unhealthy but necessary. Without it, he's crazier than ever."

Cooper shakes his head again. "That makes no sense, and I'm just thankful it wasn't me who gave him that advice because when Brook finds out, she'll be coming for you, right after she's kicked Tanner's arse." He moves towards the stairs. "Let's get changed and go with him to claim our women back."

"Harper is not my woman. I'm going to visit Willow after I've picked Kian up from Kayla and Jase's place."

"Man, you have nothing standing in your way with Harper, you can finally take her, and now you're telling me you don't want her?" he queries with amusement in his voice.

"That's what I'm saying, man. Too much has happened for us to move forward," I mutter. The feelings I had for Harper are overshadowed by the things that happened in Ginger's final days.

An hour later, Cooper knocks on Harper's front door as Tanner and I stand behind him. Brook opens the door looking freshly showered and dressed in a short, white summer dress. The minute she sees him, she pushes through to get to Tanner. He catches her in his arms when she launches herself at him and wraps her arms and legs around him, clinging to him. "I missed you so much," she mumbles into his neck. I want to slap him and tell him to remove the guilty look he's got plastered across his face before she sees it. Brook rains kisses down all over his face and finally captures his mouth in a deep kiss.

"Traitor," says Mila, stepping into the doorway and watching her friend devour Tanner.

"You ready to come home?" asks Cooper, and she eyes him for a few seconds before opening the door wider to let him in.

Asher runs to Cooper, and Cooper throws him over his shoulder and carries him into the kitchen where Mila and Harper are nursing coffees. "We had ice cream for breakfast," giggles Asher. Mila smirks up at Cooper, waiting for his reaction. He lowers himself and places a gentle kiss on her head.

"That's the best kind of breakfast," he says with a wink. "Are we going home now?"

I take a seat opposite Harper, who's feeding Willow. I love the sight of her nursing my child, it's beautiful. Cooper refuses to sit down and is using his President's voice to get Mila to get her shit together so they can go home. He wasn't happy that he spent his night next to me on the clubhouse floor rather than in bed with her. Tanner shifts uncomfortably in the kitchen doorway with Brook tucked into his side.

"You guys, we're gonna go. I need to get my man home and show him how much I've missed him," says Brook with a grin.

"See, why aren't you saying shit like that?" Cooper asks Mila.

"Enjoy," says Harper, giving the pair a wave. Mila stands and tucks her stool under the table.

"Fine, let's go home, Cooper, but it's on the condition you stop at the store on our way back to buy ice cream, lots of ice cream." Cooper groans and swats her on the backside playfully. I doubt he'll ever mention her ice cream intake ever again.

The place falls silent once everyone's left. The only sound is Willow suckling on Harper. "Do you want to take her out today? I've expressed some milk," she offers, and I scowl. She has a real obsession about me taking Willow out.

"Why do you want me out the way?"

"This is your time with her. You don't want me around." I think about her statement because as much as I can't get the whole Ginger thing out of my head, I do like being around Harper. Somehow, she calms me, and my head doesn't feel such a mess.

"I'm staying here with her. End of." Harper rolls her eyes and moves Willow over her shoulder, her breast still on show. It's wrong on so many levels, but I can't look away from her, admiring how much fuller she looks. Harper stands, tucking herself away, and rounds the table, handing Willow to me even though I have Kian on one shoulder.

"I'm gonna take a shower. Watch her." She leaves the room, and I stare down at the two bundles on my chest. They seem to settle well when they're together like this.

Harper's gone for ten minutes, and when she returns, she's looking hot with her hair still wet, her face flushed in that shy, innocent way that once lured me in. The shorts and a vest she's now wearing show off her gorgeous womanly curves. I take her in from head to toe, and she smiles at me innocently. It's all part of a game. The same one we played that got us into this mess.

"Stop," I say, a warning tone to my voice.

"Stop what?" she asks innocently.

"Whatever this is, just stop." My voice is cold. It needs to be, so she doesn't take this any further. Our lives are already complicated enough without revisiting our past.

"You seem to think everything is about you, Kain. Get over yourself." Her cheeks flush with embarrassment and she goes back upstairs.

Harper

I'm embarrassed. One night with the girls and I've come over like a desperate teenager. I confessed to them I still had feelings for Kain, that they never really went away, and the girls encouraged me to go for it, telling me he felt the same way deep down and that he just needed reminding. But the way he just shot me down tells me they're wrong. I mean, what the hell was I thinking, trying it on with the guy who's not only broken my heart over and over but treated me like shit. And on top of all that, he's just lost the mother of his son. I groan aloud, wanting the earth to swallow me whole. If he brings this up, I'll blame hormones.

I spend time blow-drying my hair, which is a luxury since having a baby. I apply a little face powder and run some light eye shadow over my lids. It's the most I've done since having Willow and I already feel better for it. The bedroom door opens and Kain pops his head in.

"Sorry," he utters, "I didn't mean to insinuate you were up to anything. My mind's crazy right now, and I have the hangover from hell." I nod, and he steps into the room. "I put the babies in Willow's bedroom. It looks amazing in there, by the way. Maybe you could come and paint a jungle on Kian's wall?" I nod again as Kain takes a seat on the end of my bed.

"Kian," I repeat with a smile.

"It was in the letter. Ginger suggested it, and I like it."

I'd forgotten about the letter, and I turn on my stool to face Kain. "You opened it?"

"Yeah, full confession in there about how she lied. It came in handy the day before my trial. She also apologised. The coroner has it now because it might help him when he does the report. She said she'd wanted to die but then discovered she was pregnant, so she waited to have Kian first." My heart feels heavy knowing she left this world even though she had a son. I couldn't imagine ever leaving Willow now.

"Would you have still wanted Kian if you'd have known she was going to leave you both?" I ask. Maybe it's insensitive, but I blurt it out before I think it through.

Kain shrugs, resting his elbows on his knees and staring down at the floor. "Maybe. I mean, he's here now and I love him, so it's hard to make that decision. I never wanted kids at all and now I have two. Would I prefer him to have his mother here? Of course. But do I regret him? No."

"Do you regret Willow?" I ask. He shakes his head, looking me in the eye. "Do you regret me?"

Kain pauses for what seems like a long time and then he sighs. "Sometimes." I bite my lower lip and nod in understanding. "I was selfish thinking I could have you both, and if I'd have done it all differently, maybe Ginger would still be here. I should have loved her more and I didn't because you were in the picture."

"Do you think she'd still be here if you had loved her more?" I ask, my voice tight from emotion.

"Yes," he says without hesitation. "I would have seen her getting worse and been able to convince her to see the doctor before she got too ill to think straight. Instead, I was fucking in dark corners with you."

I stand abruptly. "I need some air," I mutter. I push my bare feet into my running shoes, and Kain catches my hand.

"You asked the question," he says with confusion.

"I know. I guess I wasn't prepared for the truth." I pull free and leave the room, rushing down the stairs and heading straight out the door. I'm not allowed any physical exercise, so running is out of the question, but I need fresh air, so I decide on a short walk around the block.

I round the final corner to head back towards my home when I crash into a hard body. Hands steady me, and I look up. A hooded figure is holding my arms, and I frown in confusion. His grip tightens, and suddenly, I'm pushed towards a van that's parked up. I was so far in my head, I didn't notice it stop beside me. The side door is already open, and he shoves me hard. I land on my arse at the far end of the van and the door slams, leaving me in darkness. It takes a few seconds for my brain to catch up and realise what's happening. The engine starts and I scramble to my feet, yelling and banging hard on the side of the van.

It stops after a few minutes of me yelling and I freeze, wondering where we are because we haven't been driving for long. The side door opens and the figure steps inside, grabbing my arm and hauling me towards him. He slaps me hard across the face and the burn it leaves on my skin momentarily stuns me. Shoving me to the floor, he towers over me. I watch as he pulls a cloth and a small bottle from his back pocket.

"Who are you? I think you've made a mistake, my name is—" His hand dashes out and he grips my throat tight, shutting me up. He squeezes until I cough violently, trying to take a full breath. I claw at his strong hands, and then he presses the cloth to my face and I have no choice but to inhale the toxic liquid. It burns my throat, and my eyes begin to water. He releases me, shoving me hard, and I smack my head on the floor of the van. Suddenly, my eyes feel heavy and I blink until it's too hard to pry them open again.

CHAPTER TWENTY

Kain

"No, Pres, seriously, I think something bad has happened." I know Cooper is pissed because I've interrupted his making up time with Mila, but Harper's been gone for two hours now. I know she wouldn't have just gone off the radar without her purse or money. "Willow is due her feed anytime now. Harper wouldn't just leave her."

"Right, okay, give me time to get the guys together and we'll come over to you and begin a search."

I pace while I wait. Willow wakes for her feed, and I root around in the fridge. I find a couple of bottles that Harper must have expressed. She'd said she was trying to get her to take a bottle, so I warm one and feed Willow. She sucks harder than her brother, and I watch her closely for similarities.

I hear the rumble of motorcycles as my brothers arrive and I let out a sigh of relief. If anyone can locate Harper, it's these guys. Cooper is first through the door with Mila by his side. "Has she turned up?" he asks, and I shake my head.

"Something's wrong," Mila says, looking up at Cooper. "Kain's right, she wouldn't leave Willow, no matter how upset she was."

"So, think, where could she be? Who's been upset with her lately?" asks Cooper, taking a seat opposite me. I shrug my shoulders because I honestly don't know. It's not like we've been chatting too much lately.

I look to Mila for the answers, and she looks deep in thought. "Her father's been an arse lately."

I know he wasn't happy about Harper having a child with me, but he's her father and I can't imagine him hurting Harper, even if he does sound like a bully. "Maybe that's the place to start asking questions," I suggest.

"I doubt he'll talk to you guys. I'll call him and see if he's heard from her first," says Mila, pulling out her mobile. She leaves the room to make the call.

"I don't think her father's got anything to do with this, Pres," I say. "He's a complete arse, but he's all about himself."

"Well, we don't have much else to go on. Didn't she mention anything to you about where she might go, or if she had another friend we don't know about? Could she have met a guy?"

The thought has me balling my fists in anger, but I don't think Harper would leave Willow without at least calling to let me know her routine. "Nah, she hinted she was still into me earlier. If she was meeting a guy, she would have told me just to get a reaction. Besides, why wouldn't she answer her phone?" The front door opens, and Tanner comes in holding up what looks like a mobile phone.

"Pres, we found this just around the corner. It's Harper's," he says, handing it to Cooper. My heart skips a beat. Now, I know something bad has happened.

"Okay, let's not panic. Tanner, get Brook to call around the local hospitals and check there's been no accidents. There could be an innocent explanation."

Mila comes back into the room looking worried. "So, I spoke to her father. He said he hasn't seen her at all today, but he said his stepson made some threats against Harper. He then went off-radar for a few weeks. He's given me an address where Anton usually stays. He's heading over here now to help."

Harper never mentioned any of this to me. I stand, angry with myself because she should have been able to approach me with shit like that, and I've been so pre-occupied with other shit that I've let her down.

"Why did he threaten Harper?" I ask.

"He discovered that she'd known about her father's affair. He blamed her and said he would make her and her father pay for it."

Harper struggled with that secret. She didn't deserve her stepbrothers' anger. "Let me see the address," I growl, taking a piece of paper from her. It's not too far from here, and I look to Cooper. "Shall we go and check this out?"

Cooper shakes his head. "Let's see what her old man has to say first. We need the facts."

"Fuck the facts, Pres. What if he's hurt her?" I yell.

Cooper sighs and then turns to two of the prospects. "Go to the address and do a drive-by, see if the place looks alive, and then call it in." I hand the piece of paper to them, praying they find Harper unhurt.

Harper

"Finally, she wakes," says a voice from somewhere nearby. My vision is blurred, and I have a pounding headache. My mouth feels so dry that I daren't swallow. I feel around and realise I'm on something soft, maybe a bed. I try to move, but my ankles are tied together. I blink to clear my vision, but the room is so dimly lit that it doesn't really help, and then a figure comes into view. He looms over me and then pulls his hood back. I stare into the cold eyes of Anton.

I wriggle my hands behind my back to see if I can loosen the ropes that are cutting into my skin. I feel like I'm in a movie scene because quite honestly, this shit doesn't happen in real life. We're at my parent's apartment. Anton sits nearby with his head in his hands and a gun by his feet.

"Why are we here?" I ask again, because each time before, he's ignored me. My father is apparently out of town, but I know my mother didn't go with him this time so I'm not sure if she's staying at this apartment or if she's flown out to our holiday home. It's very rare that she remains in this country, but my thoughts are answered when I hear a key turn in the lock and the door opens. My mother enters the apartment, laughing at something her carer is saying as he trails behind her carrying shopping bags.

Anton makes a grab for the gun and stands, pointing it at them. My mother freezes and then laughs aloud. "Oh my god, aren't you the guy I met in that bar a few weeks ago?" she shrills. Her eyes fall to me, and she frowns in confusion. "Darling, what are you doing here?"

I wonder why that's her question and not 'darling, why are you here tied up?' "I'm not sure, Anton hasn't told me."

The carer steps in front of my mother, eyeing Anton warily. "What do you want?" he asks.

Anton shakes the gun to me. "She's got something to tell you." His voice comes out shaky, and I think this may the first time he's held a gun. His eyes are wild, and his hair is sticking up in all directions from where he's been tugging it. "Tell her," he yells at me. He grips my upper arm and pulls me to my feet. I'm bound at the ankles, so I stumble unsteadily, landing with my stomach against the table. A pain rips through me as I feel my stitches tug and I'm pretty sure I've burst a couple.

"What was your name again?" asks my mother brightly. She doesn't seem fazed at all by the gun that shakes in Anton's hand.

"Anton. His name is Anton," I say. Anton grips me by the hair and pulls my head back hard.

"Don't say my fucking name," he yells.

"Don't be ridiculous. We've had sex, darling, I need to remember your name." My mother laughs.

"Just stop talking," yells Anton. "Now, tell her about your precious father."

I sigh in frustration. I don't know why he feels the need to pull my hair. I make eye contact with my mother and say, "Mum, Dad's having an affair." Anton looks satisfied as he glares at my mother, but her face remains blank, a confused smile still pasted on her pink glossed lips.

"Is that what all of this is about?" she asks and then laughs. "Oh, really, put the gun down, Anton."

"Mother, this isn't a joke. He really is having an affair. This is Anton, his stepson."

Anton grips my hair tighter. "He is not my stepfather," he growls, and I wince as the roots of my hair tighten.

"But I know all of this," says my mother, laughing again, and I stiffen at her confession. "I've known from the beginning."

I inhale and another sharp pain rips through my stitches. I stand slightly and shove hard at Anton. He falls away, landing on his arse, and the gun clatters across the floor away from him and under a side unit. "You knew?" I hiss.

"Well, yes," says my mother, "of course, I did. He can't keep a secret that big without me guessing. I'm not blind, Harper."

"But I've kept that secret since I was a child. Dad threatened me for years. If you knew, why the hell didn't you leave him?" I yell. I turn to Anton, who looks just as shell-shocked. "Get the fuck up and un-tie me, you idiot," I snap.

My mother's carer rushes forward and begins to untie my wrists. "I couldn't leave him. I have a good life," Mum explains, and my palms itch to slap her. I've lost count of all the times I cried myself to sleep as a child feeling heartbroken for her.

"He has children with another woman," I say, and still, she doesn't react.

"More fool him," she says with a shrug. "Meanwhile, I lead a fantastic life."

"You selfish cow," I snap. "How could you bring me into such a toxic relationship? I've watched him treat you like crap for years thinking you were trapped here, and all this time, you knew, you chose to stay. Do you realise he gets him to mess with your meds?" I ask accusingly, pointing to her carer. She laughs again and then wraps her arms around her carer's waist.

"Sweetie, I haven't been medicated for many years." She places a kiss on his cheek, and he smiles down at her. My stomach forms a knot at the lies that are coming to light. I feel as if my whole life was one big lie.

"So, you two are . . ." I trail off and shake my head in disgust. My father has been paying Carlos to take care of my mother for years. He's been on family holidays and travels everywhere she goes and he's been her lover all along. "But you slept with him," I say, pointing to Anton, who is still on the floor watching the exchange.

"Well, it's a very open relationship," she says with another laugh. I reach down to untie my ankles, wincing as the pain increases. There's blood across my top, and when I stand, I gently lift it to see that two stitches have burst open.

"So, now what?" I ask Anton. "What do you want now?"

"I just want it all to stop, the lies, the cheating," he mutters pitifully. He reminds me of a child. It's how I felt years ago.

"You and me both," I snap. "You've had me here for hours. I have a newborn baby waiting for me and a biker who will slit your damn throat for this." I point to the blood that's soaking my top. My day's been hell and I just want to get home to my baby.

Pounding on the door interrupts my thoughts. I know it will be him, and when there's a bang followed by heavy footsteps, I almost smile at the dramatics of the entrance. Within a second, the apartment is full of bikers, all looking pissed and ready for a fight. Kain sees me and pulls me to him, wrapping his arms around me and burying his nose into my hair. He inhales deeply and releases it slowly. "Thank fuck," he whispers.

"What the hell's going on?" booms Cooper.

"It's a long story, Mr. President," I say with a smirk. I pull back from Kain, and when he spots the blood, his eyes widen. "Calm, it's just my stitches," I say with a smile. I lift my top and show him.

"I want a name," he grits out, and I point to Anton, who sits cowering on the floor.

"But you can't hurt him," I add with a shrug.

"To hell I can't," growls Kain, moving towards him. Anton scrambles away until he hits the wall behind and covers his face with his arms, and I roll my eyes. I don't know why I ever thought Anton was scary.

"You really can't," I say, getting between the pair. "Gloria will be so upset, despite the fact that he deserves it," I add, glaring down at the little weasel. "He's just as messed up over my father as I am. We're all blaming the wrong people. My father is the only one responsible for this mess."

There's a deep cough and I look over to where Cooper is moving his eyes in the direction of my father. I don't think, I just move, and then my hand reaches out and slaps against his face hard. His head moves to one side, and when he brings it back to look at me, there's fire in his eyes. I can see his fingers twitching to hit me back, but there's no way he'd do that here with all these people present.

"What kind of father threatens a small girl into lying so that he can cheat on two women? With the money you have deposited in my bank, I'm getting Mum the best lawyer and she's divorcing you. She's going to take you for everything she can."

"Darling, I think you're being a little rash," my mother cuts in, and I glare at her.

"Let's not forget I'm still pissed at you for lying," I snap, and she presses her lips together. "You'll still get your great life because we'll make sure you get half of everything. We all need to move on. He has a family with small children, and he's going to dedicate his life to them now." I turn to Cooper. "Can you spare a couple of prospects to help my father get his stuff together from here? He needs to be gone today." Cooper nods and motions to Kurt and Shane.

"This isn't your decision," Father snaps.

"It is. I've spent my life lying to people I love because of your selfishness. You failed me and Mum, but you will not fail Gloria and the twins. For some reason, that woman adores you, so don't fuck it up."

I was always trying to protect my mother, thinking her mental illnesses were a reason not to upset her. To find out that she knew all along, and on top of that, her illness wasn't as bad as I thought, pisses me off, but today, it all ends. Mum can have her boyfriend and they can live here and be happy. My father can be with Gloria and spend more time with her and the girls instead of trying to split his time. In a way, Mum played him too because I'm sure if he'd have known that she wasn't that ill, then he'd have left her. I think half of his frustrations were because he felt trapped. I'm freeing us all today.

CHAPTER TWENTY-ONE

Kain

It's been a week since the incident with Harper and her family. So far, I've visited her every day because despite what she keeps saying about being fine, she needs the help with Willow. She had to go and get her stitches re-done and was told she needed to rest more.

Today, there's a party at the clubhouse. One of the Prospects, Irish, is being patched in, but we won't be there. Harper needs to rest, and to make sure she does, I've been staying at hers, despite her protests.

The week's been enlightening. Harper seems happier since sorting things out with her parents, and we've had a good week where we've chilled with the kids and watched movies all day. I'm in the spare room at night, and that's fine, but I'm beginning to feel that pull again, the one I had before it all went to shit, and I want to explore it more. So, when she comes downstairs all dressed up in a tight-fitted, short, black dress, her hair straightened perfectly so it flows down her back, and her makeup all in place, I'm a little taken aback.

"Where are you going?" I ask casually, praying to God she doesn't tell me she's about to go out on a date.

"Irish is being patched in, and Mila invited me to the clubhouse. I feel much better, so you really should consider going home."

"Aren't we staying here tonight? I got us some films," I say, leaning over to the table and holding up some DVDs. "I thought the babies could have another sleepover."

"Kain, I've told you before, stop organising my plans without talking to me. I promised Mila I'd go. She said Brook seems weird, so she wants to stage a friend-ta-vension."

"What the hell's a friend-ta-vension?"

"Where we interrogate Brook until she tells us what's going on."

"I'm sure if Brook wanted to tell you, she would. My night sounds much better," I say with a grin.

"Well, you enjoy it. If you're staying here, you can watch Willow," she says with a cheeky wink, and I dive to my feet. No way am I staying home with the babies while she parties.

"I thought that would get you moving," she adds with a laugh.

"The girls are staging a friend-ta-vension," I repeat to Cooper. He looks just as baffled as I did, which I'm pleased about. "Did Tanner say anything to her?"

Cooper shakes his head. "No, but he's struggling with it all. He looks miserable and he's not being his usual stalkerish self. It wouldn't surprise me if she's noticed something weird."

"He's going to give the game away if he isn't careful. Can't you talk to him?" I ask, and Cooper nods towards the door where Tanner is. He spots us and makes his way over.

"Let's do it together. I'll let you take the lead," says Cooper with a smirk, and I give him my best annoyed look.

"Tanner, what the hell is going on, brother?" I ask as he sits on a barstool by Cooper. "Brook's miserable, you're miserable, I don't understand."

"I hate myself, brother," says Tanner, sighing. "It's not me. I don't do that shit, and now, I feel as guilty as fuck. I can't look at her, I can't have sex with her, the guilt is tearing me apart."

I roll my eyes. "Christ, Tanner, pull yourself together. We know you didn't mean it. You have to move forward. Forget about it and move on."

"It's not that easy, man. I betrayed Brook and I love her so much, man, it's killing me. I'm not like you guys. I can't be that guy."

"Then finish with her, end the relationship, because what you're doing now is just as cruel," says Cooper, and I nod in agreement.

Tanner looks horrified. "I can't let her go. She's mine."

"Then tell her the truth and see how she takes it. Maybe she'll forgive you and you can move on," suggests Cooper.

"No! Hell no, don't do that," I almost yell. "I don't wanna lose my balls over this too."

"The thing is," says Tanner, "Melissa, won't leave me alone. She's flirting her arse off and it's distracting me."

I laugh, and he looks at me innocently. "So, you're telling me that you fancy Melissa?"

"No. Well, I don't know . . ." He trails off. "I love Brook, and I want to spend the rest of my life with her."

"But you want to fuck Melissa?" I ask.

"Damn, you make it sound so much worse than it is. I'm just saying when a pretty girl like that flirts her arse off, you can't help but notice."

"Man, I'm out of this conversation. As your President, I don't want to be involved in the drama. Not to mention that my ol' lady will have my balls if I advise you wrong." We watch Cooper leave and then I turn to Tanner.

"I'm not gonna tell you what to do, cos with my history, I'm not qualified to, but if I could do it all again, I wouldn't have had two women on at the same time. The lies are too much. But if you plan to stay with Brook, then you have to weigh up whether telling her the truth now will ruin your future together."

Harper

Mila was right, Brook looks out of sorts. Usually, she'd walk in a room and light it up, but today, she looks so sad and distant. I place a bottle of beer down in front of her and a Coke for me and Mila. "So, have you heard from your parents or Anton?" asks Mila, and I shake my head. I arranged for my mother to see a lawyer the very next day after the incident, which she did. Gloria has left a few messages for me to go there for dinner, but it doesn't feel right just yet, so I told her that I was pissed with my father about his reaction to Willow's dad, but I'd go see her when he was working out of town.

"I feel so hurt by it all. I protected my mum for all those years and I didn't need to." Mila pats my hand in sympathy. "Are you okay, Brook?" I ask.

Brook looks startled. She wasn't listening and only heard me say her name. "Sorry, what?"

"Are you okay?"

"Not really." She stops and sighs. "Something's wrong with Tanner. He's acting really strange, and I just know that something's wrong."

"I take it you asked him," says Mila.

"Yeah, but he said it's nothing, club business."

"Well, maybe it is. You know what these guys are like. They get lost in the bad shit sometimes," I say. Willow wakes and begins fussing. Thanks to Kain, I feel more confident to feed her in public, so I skilfully put her to my breast and cover her with a blanket. I notice that Brook is watching wistfully, and a pang of sadness hits me. "Was he okay before you left him for the night?" I ask, wondering whether his mood has to do with the knowledge that they can't have kids.

"I know what you're thinking, and it isn't that. Trust me, he was happy when he realised I couldn't have children. This is something else. He can't even look me in the eye. Watch." She shouts Tanner over, and he reluctantly comes. She's right, he isn't acting like he normally would. For one, he was at the bar with the guys and not staring at Brook like usual.

"The girls are thinking of going away for a weekend, somewhere crazy like Vegas. That's okay with you, right, if I go?" she asks with a sweet smile. Tanner shrugs his shoulders like he couldn't give a shit and then nods in confirmation that she's free to go. "Some of the club girls are gonna come, so it'll be wild," she adds. Tanner fakes a smile that doesn't reach his eyes and then kisses her on the top of her head before going back to the guys.

Brook lowers herself into her chair, her eyebrows raised in an 'I told you so' manner. "Someone broke Tanner," I say, shocked.

"It's like he's stopped caring. I don't understand," says Mila.

"We haven't had sex in over a week. He was a two or three times a day kind of guy before, and now, nothing." We all fall silent, trying to work out why Tanner's acting so odd, but I really have no clue. "Maybe he doesn't want to be with me anymore?" she adds sadly.

"That can't be it. He's obsessed with you," says Mila.

"Perhaps threaten to leave him?" I suggest. "It may get him talking."

"But what if he lets me go?" she asks, her voice almost a whisper. An hour ago, I'd have said that would never happen, but after seeing the way he was just now, I'm not so sure.

"I hate to say it, sweetie, but maybe Harper is right. If he doesn't stop you, then you know the answer, and it's a huge gamble, but you can't carry on like this," says Mila.

Marshall joins us with his new girlfriend, Neve. I met her once when he brought her around for a coffee. She's lovely but a little quiet, though I put that down to nerves. I pass Willow over to Marshall and relax back in my chair. I've always loved being around the Hammers MC, it's a place I feel safe and wanted, and I want Willow to have this every day. I want her to have a place where she can come no matter what, with thirty or so big brothers who would die for her. Looking around now at the families all relaxing together, it brings a smile to my face.

"Harper, you'll dance with me, won't you?" shouts Woody. He's drunk and swaying in the middle of the room to a song he just put on the juke box.

"Sure, big guy, but don't step on my toes," I warn as I approach. Woody and I have been known to dance the night away a few times back when I was working the bar here. I laugh as he grips me in his strong arms and begins moving me around the dance floor. Most of the time, I'm off my feet, which is a good thing because his clumsy steps are dangerous. I catch Kain watching from his seat at the bar, and if I'm not mistaken, that's the look he used to give me back when he'd get jealous. It sends a thrill through me as I continue to dance in Woody's arms.

Kain

I stop the car outside Harper's and grip the steering wheel until my fingers turn white. I'm not hiding the fact that I'm pissed. "I thought you were staying over," she says as she reaches into the back to unclip Willow's car seat.

"Nope," I grit out.

"Right, okay. Well, I'll see you tomorrow maybe?" she asks, and when I don't reply, she closes the door. I watch her walk up her path and then decide that I'm not ready to just stop arguing, so I get out of the car and lean on the door.

"It was irresponsible. You can't just be dancing with other men when our daughter is with you," I say. Harper whips around to face me, a scowl on her beautiful face.

"Excuse me?" she snaps. I know she heard me, and she's daring me to repeat it.

"I know she doesn't see it now, but as she gets older, she will. You need to set an example." I'm pushing her buttons, and it's intentional because I love the fire in her eyes and the way her cheeks flush when she's mad.

"How dare you," she whisper-hisses, glancing around to make sure her neighbours aren't around. "I wasn't even drunk. I was having fun."

"That makes it worse. At least if you were drunk, there'd be an excuse." Harper unlocks her front door and goes inside, ignoring my comment.

"Come on, little man, let's go and piss your sister's mummy off," I whisper to Kian as I unfasten his car seat. Harper left the door unlocked, so I go straight inside. I find her in Willow's bedroom laying her down in the cot. I lay Kian on the change mat and begin getting him ready for bed. Harper eyes me suspiciously before sighing loudly and then leaving the room.

Once Kian is ready, I lay him next to Willow and pray that his last feed was enough to see him through for another couple of hours so I can get some alone time with Harper.

She's in her bedroom, sitting on the end of her bed and texting furiously on her mobile. She looks up when I enter. "What?" she asks,

"I'm jealous," I say, kicking off my heavy boots.

"They're your brothers and we were just dancing," she says, almost pouting.

"Dancing with the mother of my child. I didn't like it." I say it with force, and she chews her lower lip. I pull off my leather kutte and lay it on a chair in the corner of her room followed by with my jeans and T-shirt.

"Are you staying over?" she asks with a smirk, and I nod, knowing she isn't going to turn me away. Spending this last week with her and Willow has brought me a peace that I never thought I could have, and each night when I've forced myself to sleep in that damn single bed in the next room, it's been hard. I'm not fighting it anymore. There's nothing to stand in our way.

Harper goes for a shower, and I lay back in her bed, flicking through the channels on the television. "Brook is so upset. Has Tanner said anything to you about not wanting to be with her anymore?" she shouts through to me, and I wince. I don't want to lie, but I can't tell her the truth because it's not my place.

"No, but we thought he was acting weird. What did she say?" I ask.

"Just that he's not himself. She thinks he wants to finish things with her, so I think she's going to get in there first." My heart aches for the poor guy because I know he doesn't want that, but like Cooper said, if he can't live with the guilt, there's only one way the relationship will go.

Harper comes back into the bedroom freshly showered with a towel around her. "It's their business, baby. We can't get involved in it because then it'll become our drama."

"I like how you presume you can stay in my bed tonight," she says, raising her eyebrow to me.

"Well, I was thinking how we never laid in a bed together before, never got to spend a night in comfort together, so why can't we give it a go?" She sits on her side of the bed and runs a comb through her wet locks.

"A week ago, you turned me down," she says.

"A week ago, you said you weren't propositioning me," I counter with a smirk.

"I wasn't," she says innocently, her cheeks flushing red.

I take her comb and twist my body around so I can run it through her hair. "I know we keep dancing around the issues, Harper, but I think it's obvious how we both feel." She starts to protest but stops when I narrow my eyes in annoyance. "No more games. I've hurt you so much and you've still been there for me and Kian. I don't deserve you, I know I don't, but here we are, both single, both with kids, and both a little wiser than we were the first time around. Maybe we can salvage something here?"

"I don't know if my heart can take much more, Kain," she whispers.

I place the comb on the side table and wrap her hair around my fist. I've missed the way it feels gripped in my hand. I tug her head back slightly and capture her neck in my teeth, gently biting and then following it up with a lick to ease the sting. She keeps her eyes closed as I hook a finger in the towel where it knots around her back and tug it until it falls away.

"I miss you," I whisper, brushing my lips against her neck. I use my other hand to run light strokes up and down her waist. Her skin prickles and her nipples stiffen.

"I miss you too," she says. I use her hair to turn her head so that she faces me side on, and her eyes flick open just as I place my lips against hers in a hungry kiss. I feel her press a hand to my chest and I pull back to look at her. "What are we doing?" she asks quietly. She's uncertain and scared, and I don't blame her. I've been blowing hot and cold for months.

"I want you," I say.

"For how long, Kain? Tonight, a day, a week? I don't mind what the answer is, but I need to be clear because if it's just tonight, I need to pre-warn my heart," she mutters.

I smile down at her, pressing a gentle kiss to the tip of her nose. "Try forever," I say, and her eyes lock with mine. "Forever," I repeat because I know she doesn't believe me. "Me, you, Kian, and Willow. Forever."

CHAPTER TWENTY-TWO

Harper

My heart swells with hope. I want forever. I want it with him and the babies more than anything. The last week has been amazing, and I've not wanted to let them go each night. When he followed me in here tonight, my heart did a little happy dance. I get onto my knees and face him, not bothering to hide my naked body and the fact that my scar is still healing or that I now have stretch marks from our daughter.

"We're gonna get married," he says firmly, and I laugh.

"That wasn't very romantic, Kain," I say, kissing him. My tongue dips into his mouth, and I savour the whiskey and smoke on his breath. It's a taste I'll never get tired of.

"Because I'm not asking you to marry me, I'm telling you. I'm booking the church for the next available date, and we're doing it. No arguments. The sooner, the better."

"Should we rush it? After everything that's happened, maybe we should take our time, have a long engagement." I'm teasing him, and he knows it. He flips me onto my back, and I squeal as he pounces on top of me.

"Woman, we are getting married as soon as there's a slot. That could be tomorrow, next week, or a month, but it's happening." I don't get to answer because he thrusts into me in one fluid movement and fucks me senseless until all I can do is nod in agreement.

Kain

As it happened, I had to wait two months to get her up the aisle, and it's been the longest two months of my life. Harper wasn't too fussed on the wedding arrangements, but Mila was a force to be reckoned with, and so here I am at the altar, waiting for my wife-to-be to join me. Cooper is by my side smirking because now he gets to watch me waiting anxiously.

"Your wife spent a fortune on my wedding," I grumble, and Cooper laughs.

"Don't even compare. My wedding almost bankrupted me. We need to start dealing in weapons again just to claw it back," he jokes. "Besides, you should have put your foot down and told her no."

I look at him like he's grown an extra head because Harper is just like Mila in that respect, neither like the word 'no' and he damn well knows it. "I never thought I'd be standing here, brother," I finally say, and Cooper pats me on the back.

"We're growing up, VP. It feels great, doesn't it?" he asks, and I nod because it really does feel amazing.

Since telling Harper we were getting married, I haven't really left her side. Last night was the first time I was away from her and the babies and it just about killed me. At one point, Tanner had to stand in the doorway to stop me leaving the clubhouse to go to them. I glance over to where he sits on his own. He looks sad and lost, but he hasn't left Brook, and she hasn't left him. And although things haven't improved, at least they're still together.

"I'm so tired," moans Cooper, rubbing at his beard. Mila gave birth to his son just a couple weeks ago. "Noah likes to be attached to his mummy most of the night. I swear, she feeds him and ten minutes later he's back on her again."

"That's what breastfed babies do. Harper said Willow used her as a comforter ninety percent of the time." I laugh, and Cooper looks to me for an explanation. "I can't believe we're talking babies and breastfeeding, Pres. We've turned into pussies."

"Pussies who love our ol' ladies and their breasts, even if they're mainly for feeding our babies these days." I laugh again and nod in agreement.

The music starts up and everyone stands. Harper's father sits in the front row with Gloria. Harper didn't ask him to walk her down the aisle because things are still raw between the two. Instead, she asked Asher to walk down beside her. Her mother was in the Bahamas on holiday, so she couldn't make today. Harper said she wasn't bothered, but deep down, I think she was hurt.

I admire my wife-to-be. Her fitted wedding dress shows off her amazing curves, and all I can think about is peeling it from her body later tonight. The train of her dress is being held up by Libby and Bella, her father's twin girls, and following behind them is Brook and Mila. She takes each step super slow, and when she's less than a foot away, I march to her. "Get a move on," I say firmly, and everyone giggles as I pull her the rest of the way.

We exchange vows, and I just want to get to the part where we put the rings on and kiss because then I know that she's mine.

When it's time for the kiss, I practically eat her at the altar as the church fills with whoops and cheers. "I love you, Mrs. Morgan," I whisper against her lips.

She smiles. "I love you too, Mr. Morgan."

Harper

Nobody tells you that you spend a fortune to get married so that everyone else can enjoy the party while you sweat your arse off in a dress that squeezes and pinches every inch of skin. Then, you smile and pose for a million different photographs when actually all you really want to do is turn off the smile, put on something comfortable, and get drunk while dancing with your new husband.

Kayla is having the babies overnight, which means I can have a drink and relax, but I've yet to feel the benefits because people keep stopping to congratulate me. I finally get away from Gloria and find Mila and Brook at the bar. I snatch a glass of Champagne from a tray, even though I hate the stuff, and knock it back in one large gulp.

"So, tell me what's going on," I demand, because they looked like they were deep in conversation. Mila hesitates, which only intrigues me more.

"I think Tanner is having an affair," blurts out Brook, and I almost snort the Champagne back through my nose.

"He would never do that, Brook. He loves you," I reassure her.

"He's taking me to dinner tomorrow to discuss something. I think he's going to confess and then dump me."

"I'm sure he's not, but dinner and a chat to clear the air sounds good. This has been going on for too long," I say, squeezing her arm.

There's a commotion and Tanner runs into the bar following a club girl. She hasn't been around for the last few weeks, and I don't recall her name, but she looks so pissed right now that I wouldn't want to be on the receiving end of her anger. She stops in front of Brook just as Tanner reaches us with the guiltiest expression I have ever seen on a man. And I know . . . I just know what's about to happen and there's not a thing I can do to stop it.

"Brook, we need to go," he says, his voice higher pitched than normal. Brook folds her arms over her chest and eyes the girl before her suspiciously. She then looks to Tanner, waiting for him to explain. He shakes his head, silently begging her to go with him.

"What do you want?" Brook asks the girl.

"To tell you something," she says with an attitude that riles me.

"Mel, I'm begging you, please don't. Not here, not today," says Tanner, his tone turning to desperation. I note the shortened version of her name that Tanner used and it confirms my suspicions.

"Tanner, be quiet," snaps Brook, and he groans, putting his head in his hands.

"I slept with him," says Melissa boldly. I hear Brook's sudden intake of breath followed by a look of pure devastation on her face. It's one thing suspecting it but a whole other having it confirmed.

"I don't think we should do this here," I whisper, noting that the guests are beginning to quiet down and look our way. Brook holds up her hand to shush me, and I press my lips together.

"When?" she asks Melissa.

"A few months ago," says Melissa with a shrug. To her, it was just sex and she isn't bothered recalling the facts, but to Brook, those details are important. Her eyes find Tanner's, and he sighs heavily.

"When you left me that night to clear your head."

"Where?" asks Brook coldly.

"Does it fucking matter where?" he suddenly snaps.

"Yeah, it does, Tanner," she hisses, not at all phased by his attitude.

"On a couch in the clubhouse. I don't even remember it." He places his hands on his hips, frustration rolling off him. He's backed into a corner and he hates it.

"Anyway, that's not what I came to tell you," says Melissa, her patience wearing thin at the mini row between Brook and Tanner. "I'm pregnant."

The world stops turning and the voices around us seem distant and echoey. Tanner's face crumbles with the pain that he knows Brook is feeling. Brook cries out, her hands cover her mouth, and she bends at the knees so that she's crouching to the floor. Her head is buried in her hands, and I hear her taking deep breaths as the news settles that Tanner is having the baby that she so desperately wanted, but with someone else.

"Brook, please, I'm so sorry," cries Tanner, bending down in front of her.

"No," screams Mila suddenly, shoving at Tanner so he falls back onto his arse. "Get out of my sight," she yells.

I glance at Mila, and we're both crying silent tears as our friend falls apart. I crouch beside her, wincing as my dress pinches some more. "Honey, we need to move. Let's get you out of here." I help her to stand and lead her away. There's a commotion that has Cooper and Kain running towards where we left Tanner on the ground. We go into Cooper's office, locking the door.

"Shit," I finally say, glancing at the other two in shock.

"It hurts to breathe," Brook whispers, rubbing at her chest.

"I think it's shock, or maybe a panic attack. Just breathe slow, in through your nose and out through your mouth," I instruct, taking her hands and demonstrating. After a few calming breaths, tears begin to leak from the corners of her eyes, slipping silently down her cheeks and dropping from her chin.

"I'm so sorry about this. It's your wedding day," she whispers.

I smile softly. "Oh, sweetie, don't even think about that after the news you've just had. And besides, what's a Hammers wedding without a little drama?" I joke.

She laughs through her tears and then begins to sob. Her whole body shakes, and my heart breaks all over again for her.

"I'm in shock," whispers Mila. "Not Tanner, he's a good one."

"Is it just me or does it completely shake your confidence in them all?" I ask, and Mila nods in agreement.

"I guess it makes you realise that if one of the good ones can slip up, then any of them can. Although to be fair, both of our guys have been there and done that," says Mila, and we all laugh.

"Maybe that can give you hope, Brook. If we got our men back, then you will to. Just because this bitch turns up saying she's pregnant, it doesn't mean he doesn't love you. It explains his behaviour though. Guilt," I say.

"I don't want hope. We're done. I can't ever forgive him for this. I wanted his baby so badly, and he gave it to a club whore. There's no coming back from that."

CHAPTER TWENTY-THREE

Kain

Married life should begin with husband and wife making a home together. I've been married three days, and so far, it's consisted of me sitting across the breakfast table from my new wife and her friend, Brook. Don't get me wrong, I love Brook, she's one of us and I know she needs us right now, but just once, I'd like to fuck my wife on the breakfast bar or over the couch and take full advantage when the kids are sleeping.

I watch as both women coo with the babies while I shovel toast into my mouth and think of an excuse to get the hell out of here. Maybe I can go and punch Tanner for fucking my life up too.

"I was thinking," says Brook, "I can't stay here forever." My ears prick up. Harper rushes to tell her she's welcome to stay as long as it takes, and I resist the urge to cover her mouth. "Harper, you guys are newlyweds, you need to have some privacy," argues Brook. I remain quiet because if I agree with Brook, I look like the bad guy and Harper will kick my arse, but If I agree with Harper, then we'll be stuck with Brook forever.

"Well, Kain and I were already discussing getting a bigger place, and I like having you around," says Harper. I stand, causing the chair legs to scrape across the floor, making a godawful noise.

Both women look up in surprise, and I smile awkwardly. "Harper, baby, can I have a word?" I wait until we're upstairs in the bedroom before I turn on her. "What the fuck are you talking about? Brook is not moving in permanently," I whisper-hiss.

Harper looks offended and then mad. "She's going through hell right now and she needs us, thanks to your brother."

"It's not my fault that Tanner fucked someone else, so why should I have to pay for it?" I snap. "She needs to find a place of her own so we can enjoy being married. I want to fuck my wife all over the house whenever I want to." I'm aware that I sound like a selfish prick, but short of stamping my feet, I don't know how clearer I can make myself.

"Kain, I can't kick her out. I feel guilt all the time for what we did to Ginger, and now, I have a chance to make it right by helping Brook through this," she says.

I place a gentle kiss on her head. "Baby, what happened with Ginger was my fault. You have nothing to feel guilty about, we went over this." I take a minute to come up with a new plan. "Okay, what about if Brook takes over this place? She can pay rent at a low cost until she's sorted, and we can move out to a bigger place with the babies, and everyone's happy?"

Harper smiles and nods in agreement. "I like that idea," she says.

"Great, let's go and tell her the plan, and then I'll get house hunting." I place a lingering kiss against her soft lips and take her hand to lead her back downstairs. I already have a house in mind that's near the clubhouse.

Later, I put a call through and offer the asking price for a quick move.

CHAPTER TWENTY-FOUR

Harper

It may have taken us a long time to get here, but as I flop down on the new sofa in our new home, I feel so happy, I could burst. Kain managed to get us a fantastic four-bedroom home not too far from the clubhouse, which I was ecstatic about because I get to spend more time with Mila and baby Noah. I stare at the framed photograph on the wall that Kain just finished putting up. It's a professional one we had done of the babies. A lady came out especially to do it for us, and she was amazing. Willow is snuggled in the middle with Noah and Kian on either side of her, and Asher is curled around them all. We often joke about how hard Willow's going to have it with the boys watching over her.

Tanner places a box on the living room floor and waits for me to acknowledge him. When I don't, he sighs heavily. "How long will you keep this up for?"

"Until Brook forgives you, which will never happen, so . . ." I let the sentence trail off. Mila is giving him the same treatment.

"I don't get it. Kain and Cooper treated you and Mila bad, and you came around. I fuck up and everyone hates me."

"Because it isn't you, Tanner. Your betrayal hurt the most because we never thought you could do that. You were besotted with Brook, and you hurt her in the worst possible way," I say sadly.

"You don't think I know that?"

"Are you planning on a happy ever after with Melissa?" I ask, fearing the answer in case I have to break the news to Brook.

"No, there's nothing between me and Melissa. I can't force her to get rid of the baby, but I've made it clear that's what I want. I love Brook and I'll spend the rest of my life making it up to her, I promise." I know he's sincere. He's been following Brook around, much to her annoyance. She's ignored him in the hope he'll get bored, but I have a feeling his love for her runs too deep.

"You're wasting your time, Tanner. She hates you." It's blunt and I see the pain in his eyes, but she really is done. She is insistent that there is no chance of her forgiving him for this, and I don't blame her.

"What's going on in here? It all sounds serious," says Kain, coming from the kitchen.

"I was telling your friend here that he's wasting his time with Brook. She's moving on, she doesn't want to have anything to do with the club, and he really needs to stop following her around."

Kain looks to Tanner. "Man, I thought I told you to stop following her. It's weird, and you'll end up inside for stalking."

"I can't help it, VP. She's mine, and I need to be around her."

"Christ, Tanner, listen to yourself. Stay the fuck away from her. Go fuck Melissa until Brook is out of your system." I slap Kain on the arm. I do not want Tanner going to Melissa, as that'll send Brook over the edge.

"It's time to get everyone out of here and lock the doors. I need to get my babies to bed and worship my wife's body," says Kain with a smirk.

"Okay, Tanner, get everyone out. Thanks for your help," I say, following him to the door. There is nothing I need more right now than to be locked in my new home with my new husband and our two children. I'll make sure that Kian grows up knowing all about his mother—it's the least I can do for Ginger after what I put her through, but I can't spend the rest of my life feeling guilty for it. I love Kian just like he's my own, and I'm excited to see where our new life as a family will take us, now that I finally have my man.

The End

Tanner – The Splintered Hearts Series

Take a sneak peek at what's to come...

CHAPTER ONE

Tanner

"Tanner, I need you on this, where the fuck are you?" demands Cooper, my club President. "I'm sick of having to track you down. You don't answer my calls. You don't check in. What use is an Enforcer if he's never around?"

I sigh. He's grating on me with his nagging wife rants. Of course, I'm off radar, cos I just lost the love of my life and the last thing I wanna do is collect debts for the club. Movement from the apartment catches my eye. "Look, Pres, can I call you back? I'm in the middle of something," I say in a quiet voice.

"No, Tanner, you can't fucking call me back. Get your arse back to the club. We need a chat." He disconnects the call, and I shove the mobile back in my pocket. Fuck Cooper. He might be my Pres, but he needs to give me a break and see the shit I've got going on right now. The door to her place opens and I step back into the shadows. The last thing I need is her to call the Polices on me again.

"I swear you do it on purpose," her voice rings out into the empty street. She's smiling. I miss that smile. Brook, my ex, my world. She looks amazing in her tight-fit denim jeans, low cut white shirt, and leather jacket. She wears her hair different these days. It's longer and shapes her face better.

"I do not. It was a last-minute decision. James was feeling low, and I thought to myself, what's the best way to cheer him up? You could have said no," replies Henry Edge, owner of Edgy Cuts Hair Salon. Gay, single, and thirty years old, Henry is Brook's new boss and, from the amount of time they spend together, I'd say new best friend.

"Me, turn down a night out, erm, as if." She laughs again, and my heart aches. I want to make her laugh like that again. I'd give anything.

I follow them, staying back in the shadows until they reach their destination—a small wine bar just around the corner from Brook's new place.

My mobile vibrates in my pocket, but I wait for them to go inside the bar before answering. "You'd better be on your way, Tanner," comes Cooper's pissed-off voice for a second time.

"I told you, I'm busy right now. I'll be there as soon as I can."

"Are you watching her again?" he presses. I keep quiet, not wanting to lie to my President but not wanting to reveal the truth either. "You know what, don't even answer that because it'll make me want to kick your arse even more. Melissa has turned up here looking for you, and unless you want my ol' lady to start hunting you down, I suggest you get back here. The ol' ladies are already staring Melissa down. It's like a damn witch hunt, and I don't wanna be the referee in your clusterfuck."

"Cooper, can't you have a word with them? I can't be there just yet." Melissa can handle her own. She won't be upset by the ol' ladies being bitchy, but she won't be happy having to wait around for me, especially as I'd been avoiding her calls all week. I need to make sure Brook gets home safe before I even think of leaving.

"No, I can't! Get back here or I'll tell Melissa exactly where you are and what you've been doing, and then I'll tell Mila that you're still stalking one of her best friends."

"Great, thanks for nothing, Pres." I disconnect the call, in temper. I get a glimpse of Brook through the bar window. Since starting her new job, she's made new friends, pushing the Hammers MC firmly out of her life. Most of the ol' ladies hold me responsible for that, and I don't blame them. It's totally my fault. I got drunk and cheated on Brook with Melissa, a nineteen-year-old club whore, and then to add insult to injury, Melissa turned up a few months later announcing that she was pregnant. Brook wants a child so desperately, but she's been told by doctors that she can't conceive naturally.

So, now, here we are. She's moved on. Left me, left the club, and started a new life, one that doesn't involve any of us.

ele

By the time I reach the club, Cooper is waiting outside with Melissa. Her hands rest on her small bump, and the sight repulses me. I hate myself for what I've done, and that bump is a constant reminder.

I park up and make my way over, fist bumping Cooper in greeting before turning to Melissa. "Hey," I mutter, keeping my eyes lowered.

"Shit, Tanner, you can look at me, yah know. I ain't that disgusting," she snaps.

"What're you doing here?" I ask.

"I need money. I've tried calling you, but you never answer. What if something happens to the kid and I need you?" she demands. I want to tell her that I wouldn't care, which makes me an arse, but it's how I feel. "I even messaged Brook on social media, and the cheeky cow deleted it and then blocked my profile."

"You contacted Brook?" It immediately annoys me. The last thing Brook needs is Melissa contacting her to track me down. "Don't do that again." I pull my wallet out and take out a bunch of twenties, stuffing them in her waiting hand. "What do you need it for?"

"Baby stuff, obviously." She rolls her eyes and then marches away, flicking her hair over her shoulder as she goes. I stand beside Cooper in silence, watching as a black car slows outside the gates. Melissa gets inside and it drives away at speed.

"Aren't you worried about who she's with, what she spends the money on?" asks Cooper.

"Nope." I head inside, where a few of my brothers are playing a game of cards in the bar. Cash is piled in the middle, something I'd usually take part in, but right now, I need to shower and get back to Brook.

Mila steps in front of me, her expression hard. Since becoming Cooper's ol' lady, she's really toughened up, keeping us guys in order. "Not now, Mila. I don't have time."

I know instantly it's the wrong thing to say because her hands go to her hips and her eyes narrow. She isn't budging out of my way until she's said what she needs to, and so I drop down onto the nearest stool and sit back, waiting for the lecture to begin.

"Sit up straight," she snaps. I do it, mainly because it'll just make her speech longer if I don't. "Brook knows you're still following her. She moved to a new place to stop this bullshit and then you turn up there. It has to stop, Tanner."

"I'm making sure she's okay," I mutter feebly.

"She doesn't need you to. She's moving on."

"What does that mean?" I sit up farther, suddenly interested in the conversation.

"It means you need to stop following her. It's weird now you're not together. I mean, it was weird before but . . . well, now, it's stalkerish."

"Has she met someone else?" It'll kill me, but I need to know.

Mila doesn't meet my eyes. Instead, she knots her fingers, a sure sign she's uncomfortable. "Not yet, but she's talking about it. It's been three months now, and it's time she got back out there."

"Three months is fuck all. She loves me, she'll never be able to move on from that!" I'm angry, and my raised voice gets the attention of some of the guys. Kain, the club's VP, stands and slowly makes his way over.

"It doesn't matter if she loves you. She will never be with you now, and so getting back out there will help her move forward. Stay away from her, Tanner."

"Things good, brother?" asks Kain casually. I don't have the energy to answer. Instead, I take myself off to my room. I'll shower and get back to Brook. We need to talk.

Brook

Henry revels in matchmaking. He said it's where his expertise truly lies. So, the fact he's now chatting to the gorgeous six-foot, dark-haired man I'd glanced at ten minutes ago doesn't surprise me. Occasionally, they both look my way, and I know my face is crimson with embarrassment.

James places a tray of empty glasses down on the table and the bartender follows, adding two bottles of Champagne. It's how these guys roll. I'm a little less extravagant, coming from a poorer background. I appreciate money, and even if I could afford the ridiculously overpriced Champagne, I wouldn't buy it.

James pours me a glass, sliding it towards me. "I'll get my drink, James. You know I don't drink that stuff."

"Tonight, you can entertain my overindulgence because I'm sad and I get to boss everyone around."

I laugh, taking the glass. "Emotional blackmail is pathetic."

James is Henry's best friend. Both are gay and proud—sometimes it feels like a competition between the pair to see who's the proudest.

Henry owns a hair salon called Edgy Cuts. He opened it five years ago, and James was his very first employee. Then came William, straight and handsome. I'm sure women came to Edgy purely to have his fingers running through their hair. He's mega talented and has won awards for his styling abilities. After Will came Blake. She's ridiculously girly and, standing at five-foot-three and of slim build, she certainly ticks a lot of men's boxes. I joined the team just two months ago, and so far, I'm loving it. Everyone welcomed me, and instantly I felt like one of the family.

It'd been a few years since I've worked, because at sixteen I'd met my ex, Tanner, and he'd convinced me to finish the course I'd begun as a trainee stylist. He said I wouldn't need to work because he wanted to look after me. I was in love, and I was happy, as long as he was, so I cut hair at the MC clubhouse, which he's a member of, for the guys and their ol' ladies, but I didn't bother to chase my dream.

"Earth to Brook," says James, waving his hand in front of my face. "Male incoming."

I look over to where the handsome stranger is following Henry to our table and my face immediately flushes again. It's also been a long time since I spoke to men other than the bikers at the Hammers MC.

"Brook, this is Anton. He's thirty-two and works in a bank."

"Oh." I smile, unsure of how to respond. The guys are always pushing me to date, but I'm far too inexperienced in that scene. Plus, it's only been three months since Tanner and I broke up, we were together a long time and I'm still not sure how to function without him.

"And you work in a salon?" asks Anton, taking a seat. I nod, sipping nervously on my Champagne.

"Brook." The sound of that familiar voice causes me to spill Champagne down my chin. I swipe at it, using the back of my hand, and look up at Tanner, who towers over the table, gaining everyone's full attention.

"What are you doing here?" My voice wobbles with nerves. It's been months since I've spoken to him, but I've felt him watching me from a distance. It's like an invisible connection we have, although lately, I've not felt him and so I'm surprised to find him here, staring at me with those eyes so full of guilt and shame.

"We need to talk." He shifts awkwardly, keeping his head lowered and his hands stuffed into his pockets.

"Now's not a good time." I don't have the strength to speak with Tanner. My heart still hurts after what he's done to me.

"Now is perfect. Get up." I hear James suck in a wistful breath. I know how Tanner affects women with his muscles, his dark beard, and his tattoos, looking like the ultimate bad boy-come-Hercules, and I'm not surprised he has the same effect on my gay friend.

"Tanner, not now," I say a little more firmly. Tanner doesn't know how to deal with me when I refuse him. Months ago, when we were still in a relationship, he'd chase me around and fuck me into submission. Now it isn't an option, I can see he isn't sure how to handle the situation. It's another reminder of how we never communicated outside the bedroom.

Without another word, he turns and leaves. I can feel everyone's shocked eyes on me, but I focus on my drink, knocking back the bubbly liquid and wincing at the bitter aftertaste.

"That was Tanner?" Blake eventually squeaks. I nod, smiling when James tops up my empty glass. "Oh my god, he's hot. Why didn't you say how hot he is?"

"How are you still sitting there like nothing's happened. I'd have jumped on his retreating back and wrestled him to the ground, then stripped him and ran my tongue all over those rock-hard pecs of his," growls Henry, and I laugh. Months ago, that's probably what I would have wanted to do, but these days, I'm much more restrained because I know how much power he has to destroy me.

"Anton, how long have you been in banking?" I ask brightly. A change in topic is exactly what's needed.

Despite Henry's many attempts to get me drunk, I stopped drinking after two glasses of Champagne. Seeing Tanner changed my mood, and once everyone in the group had gotten up to dance, I'd made my excuses and left.

Anton insisted on walking me home, which I insisted was completely unnecessary, but he was so pushy about it, I gave in, and now, I have my rape alarm gripped tightly in my jacket pocket, just in case.

"I'd love to see you again, Brook," he says as we slow right outside my apartment block.

"Yeah, maybe." Things feel awkward and forced, but I take the business card he holds out for me. *Is this how people do things these days, by handing out business cards?*

"Give me a call and maybe we can arrange lunch one day next week?"

I nod, shoving the little card into my pocket. "Thanks for walking me home. Goodnight." I don't miss the disappointment on his face right before I walk up the steps, but I'm not going to kiss the guy or invite him inside. I'm a fourth date minimum kind of girl, at least, I think I am.

I use my security fob to get in, and I'm startled to see Tanner sitting on the floor of the lobby, waiting by the lift. "Tanner, what are you doing here?" I ask, sighing. My heart rate doubles, thudding hard in my chest.

"Did you kiss him? I couldn't bear to watch that, but now I need to know."

"You've been watching me again? You have to stop. Go home or I'm calling Cooper to come get you."

"Did you kiss him?" he growls, his eyes burning into my own. They're full of pain and a part of me is glad. He deserves to hurt after everything he's done. I loved him so much, and I still do. We were inseparable and intense, and we knew each other inside out. I could sense him in a crowd, we were that close. He couldn't bear to be away from me, and I guess I felt the same, which made his cheating even more painful.

"That's none of your business, Tanner. Get the fuck out." I pull out my mobile phone and hold it up in warning. I'm not afraid to rat him out to his Pres if he doesn't leave.

Tanner pushes to his feet and stuffs his hands back into his pockets. "Please, Brook. I'll beg if you want me to. Five minutes . . . just five." He's tugging on my heart strings with that lost boy look on his chiselled face. I roll my eyes in defeat and press the button for the lift.

Tanner steps in first, standing behind me. The pull between us as the doors slide closed is so intense, I squeeze my eyes shut and pray for it to move faster so I can escape the proximity. It doesn't feel right being so close and not being wrapped in his arms.

Stepping out into the passage, I turn right and unlock my apartment door. I step to one side and let Tanner go in ahead of me. He stops beside me, almost pushing against me yet not quite touching. His hands are still firmly stuffed into his pockets, and I wonder if he feels the urge to touch me too. I watch as he closes his eyes and tilts his head closer before inhaling. "You changed your shampoo," he whispers, disappointment in his tone. "You smell different."

"Your five minutes have started, Tanner," I say, keeping my voice steady. The truth is, I miss his scent too, the mix of whisky, spicy cologne, and leather. I changed mine on purpose, because he used to tell me he'd bottle it if he could, that it calmed his soul. I wanted to reinvent myself to be far from anything he could use to his advantage.

Once inside, I turn on the coffee machine and it springs to life. I set up one cup, not wanting to make him comfortable. "So," I push, "you wanted to talk."

"Are you okay?" he begins.

"You came here to ask how I am?" I scoff, glaring at him. Laughing, I shake my head in disappointment. "How do you think I am, Tanner?" It's a stupid question and it pisses me off.

"You seem okay. New job, nice apartment, new clothes, different hair, new friends, different scent." He reels off the list and then shrugs his shoulders in a sulky manner.

"Did you want to see me sitting in a corner, rocking and crying?"

"Of course not, I just . . ." He trails off.

"Because I do that too, Tanner. None of this has been easy for me." I sigh angrily. "How's Melissa?" I ask coldly. I don't give a shit about her, and he knows it, but I want to see his reaction. I'd instructed Mila and Harper not to tell me about anything club-related, especially not anything about Tanner and Melissa, but I can't help being curious. Is he in a relationship with her? Do they have a nursery set up for the baby? Do they share our old bedroom at the clubhouse? The questions run through my head, and I stir my coffee to distract myself.

"I don't want to talk about her. It isn't why I came here. We have a follow-up appointment with your gynaecologist. Did you remember?"

I laugh, hardly believing he'd dare to bring that up. We made that appointment before we split up to discuss different avenues for us to have a baby since I'd been told I can't conceive. Tanner was dead set against the idea of other avenues, but I think he agreed because he felt sorry for me. He knew I wanted kids, and when I found out that wasn't possible, it broke my heart. The truth was, Tanner didn't want to share me with anyone, not even his own baby.

"Joint appointments ended when we did, Tanner," I snap. "Your time is up, leave."

Tanner takes a mug from the dishwasher and places it on the side. He pours himself a black coffee, ignoring my request for him to go. "I think we should still go. It took us a long time to get the appointment. He was booked up for months in advance."

"Are you kidding me right now?" I snap in disbelief. "We broke up, so I don't need to talk about having a kid with you because it's impossible."

"It's not impossible," he mutters, staring into his mug. "Maybe I can still give you that."

I suck in a breath, then my chest begins to hurt again and I rub it, trying to make it stop. "What the hell are you talking about?"

"I know how badly you want a baby. I can still give you that. The doctors can do so much these days, test tube babies or planting the egg straight into your womb. I looked it up on the internet. I'll pay for whatever they can do to give you a baby."

"Oh my god, you need to leave," I mutter, shaking my head in disbelief.

"Why is it such a bad idea, Brook? You can have the baby you always wanted."

"And have you in my life forever, I don't think so."

"Is that so bad?"

"Yes, it's bad. I don't want you around as a constant reminder of how much you've hurt me, Tanner. I wanted a baby with you for so long, and you always told me it wasn't the right time. Did you have that same conversation with Melissa? Did you discuss timing and your financial situation not being stable enough?" I'm ranting, but I can't stop myself, I've bottled so much up since our split. "When we found out I couldn't have kids, my first thought was that it was your fault. Did you know that?" Tanner shakes his head, hurt clear on his face. "If I hadn't aborted our first baby because you weren't ready, then I'd be a mum now. I feel like God took away my chance because I screwed up the first miracle he gave me."

"That's not fair, Brook. You weren't ready either."

"I was ready, but I was scared I'd lose you. I was pathetic and weak, and I thought I needed you to survive. How dare you come here and offer me a baby after what you've done to me! Your life will be spent worrying about Melissa taking care of your child, because I can tell you now, she will not be a good mother. She doesn't want your baby. She doesn't want to be a mum. You picked the worst person to raise your child, and now, you have to live with that."

"This isn't you. You sound bitter and hateful and that's not the Brook I once knew. All this," he snaps, tugging at my new leather jacket, "this trendy shit you wear, it isn't you. My Brook liked summer dresses and Doc Martens boots. She loved staying home and watching movies, not going out partying every night with stuck-up bastards who drink Champagne like water. It's all fake, and you're being fake. You hardly see anyone from the club, now you prefer the company of your new work friends!" He's shouting, his face red with anger, but his tone mocking.

"Maybe this was the Brook I should have been. If I'd have been this Brook, then you wouldn't have given me a second look and my heart wouldn't hurt so much right now." I place my coffee down and head for the bathroom, locking the door behind me. I pull out my phone and dial Cooper's number.

To continue, head here... https://mybook.to/TannerSH

More books from Nicola Jane

The Kings Reapers MC

Riggs' Ruin https://mybook.to/RiggsRuin

Capturing Cree https://mybook.to/CapturingCree

Wrapped in Chains https://mybook.to/WrappedinChains

Saving Blu https://mybook.to/SavingBlu

Riggs' Saviour https://mybook.to/RiggsSaviour

Taming Blade https://mybook.to/TamingBlade

Misleading Lake https://mybook.to/MisleadingLake

Surviving Storm https://mybook.to/SurvivingStorm

Ravens Place https://mybook.to/RavensPlace

Playing Vinn https://mybook.to/PlayingVinn

The Perished Riders MC

Maverick https://mybook.to/Maverick-Perished

Scar https://mybook.to/Scar-Perished

Grim https://mybook.to/Grim-Perished

Ghost https://mybook.to/GhostBk4

Dice https://mybook.to/DiceBk5

Arthur https://mybook.to/ArthurNJ

The Hammers MC (Splintered Hearts Series)

Cooper https://mybook.to/CooperSHS

Kain https://mybook.to/Kain

Tanner https://mybook.to/TannerSH

Milton Keynes UK
Ingram Content Group UK Ltd.
UKHW020200230823
427286UK00016B/570